MW01248983

ISBN: 9798852396785

Cover design by: Steve Lance
Printed in the United States of America

GUILTY UNTIL PROVEN INNOCENT

by
Steve Lance

TABLE OF CONTENTS

1) DNA REPORT

In a fit of rage, District Attorney Robert "Duke" Billings crumbled the DNA report and flung it at Todd Baker. The report ricocheted off Todd's face and landed at his feet. Duke's arm swept across the desk, sending a coffee mug crashing to the floor. His eyes darted to the window. People in the outer office strained their necks, trying to see what was causing the commotion. He slammed the blinds shut and shoved Baker into a chair. Gripping both armrests, he leaned in until he was an inch from Baker's face. "How did you screw this up? Not only did you botch the DNA test. You screwed me over good."

Todd, trembling, sweat on his brow, pushed back into the chair, trying to create space between himself and Billings' penetrating stare. Duke Billings, who once played linebacker for The Ohio State Buckeyes, was an imposing figure, standing six foot three with broad shoulders and dark brown eyes. Todd uttered a few incoherent syllables.

Suppressing the urge to strike Baker, Duke leaned closer, his knuckles turning white, his neck bulging, his biceps straining against the fabric of his shirt. Finally, he released the chair. It skidded back a few inches, letting out a high pitch screech.

Duke turned and stared at a bookcase full of law books, deciding what to do next. At this moment, the jury was deliberating on whether to convict Jake Franklin of murder. They were most likely going to return a guilty verdict. Duke had been flawless in his prosecution, repeatedly returning to the DNA evidence, hammering the point that it showed Franklin was the murderer. He had presented other evidence, but it was all circumstantial. The DNA proved Franklin raped Suzy James and then slashed her throat.

Duke's only legitimate option was to contact the judge and have a mistrial declared. It's a simple decision if you go strictly by the book. But there was more to consider. The case had caught the attention of the national press. Reporters filled the courthouse steps, jockeying for position, waiting to shove a camera into someone's face. A mistrial would be like throwing chum into shark-infested waters. A feeding frenzy would ensue. Every newscast's lead story would be about Jake Franklin, the victim of an overzealous and incompetent District Attorney. It would destroy Duke Billings' career. Everything he had worked for would be gone in an instant.

Reporters were not interested in the details. They would ignore that a low-level lab technician botched the DNA test. While the District Attorney had presented a stellar prosecution. To them, there was no nuance. You were a winner or a loser. In their world, everything was binary. They had less than a minute to report the news. The audience didn't want a complicated story. They only needed to know who they should cheer and who they should jeer. They wanted good guys and bad guys, everything to be black and white. The reporters' hair and makeup were more important than the facts. A reporter could stare into a camera, utter a simple sentence, and destroy Duke's career.

Dressed in a black tee shirt and unkempt jeans begging for a wash, Todd Baker looked like he had just gotten out of bed. Duke scowled at him. He could have at least worn a collared shirt. The world had gone casual, but you still needed to show respect. A low-level lab technician needing a shave and a shower wasn't going to show up at the last minute and ruin Billings' career. Baker sat shaking in a chair far too large for his scrawny body. If only the chair would swallow him and make this problem vanish. Send Baker back to whatever fluorescent light, bureaucrat-infested row of cubicles he climbed out of.

Duke thought, "*Unwashed clothes, stubble on his cheek, unable to care for himself; how can you trust this fool with critical lab information? He got the results wrong once. What is to say he hasn't gotten them wrong again? I'm not letting a murderer go free because he is incompetent. No, the best course of action is to let the trial go forward. Baker had his chance. He testified the DNA results matched Jake Franklin. The jury is deliberating. If the DNA is incorrect, the defense can have it retested on appeal."*

"You testified to these results," Duke pointed an accusatory finger at Baker. "That is perjury. I can send you to prison."

Todd stumbled over his words but finally said, "I mixed up the sample numbers. It was an honest mistake."

Duke went to the office shades. He created a small opening between the slats and peered out. Nothing unusual. Everyone had returned to work. As far as they were concerned, his outburst was another in a long line of outbursts. Business as usual.

"The trial is over. It's up to the jury. I can't help you," Duke said.

"Should I go to the judge?" Todd asked. His voice cracked, and his eyes pleaded with Duke to help.

"Only if you want to be sent to prison. If I were you. I wouldn't do anything. The jury may find Franklin innocent, and the whole point becomes irrelevant."

"But what if they find him guilty?"

"That's what appeals are for. If it's not Franklin's DNA, any defense attorney worth his salt will have it retested." Duke studied Baker. It was like watching a fish flop around on the dock. He knew he was giving him poor advice. He should inform the judge. But if that happens, the judge will immediately declare a mistrial. A potential murderer would walk, and Duke's once-promising career would end.

"But in the trial, he claimed it was not his DNA, and I testified it was a match. I was wrong."

"You don't know that. Your first test said it was a match. Maybe that one was right."

"But—"

"Do you want my help?" Duke gave Todd a hard stare. "First, we never talked about this. It's improper for you and me to be having this conversation. So, keep quiet unless you want to add this along with perjury. It's for your own good. If you bring it up, I'll have no choice but to throw the book at you. Second, let the jury do their job. Franklin gave testimony, the same as you. It's up to the jury to decide."

"But my testimony was wrong."

"If that is the case. And I don't believe it is. The defense attorney will have it retested on appeal."

"No question I got the DNA wrong."

"Stop it. One day you say one thing, the next, it's something else. You don't know what the hell is going on. So, stop talking and let the jury and the defense attorney do their job." Duke walked behind Baker and put his hands on Todd's shoulders. He wanted to strangle the little punk, but needed Baker to calm down. So, instead, he gave a quick squeeze.

"Are you sure I'm doing the right thing?"

"Of course you are. Now don't say anything to anyone. And don't do anything else." Duke walked around and faced Todd. "Now get the hell out of my office," he said, half joking with a threatening undertone.

Todd took a few tentative steps toward the door. Duke motioned with his hand for him to continue, trying to sweep Todd and his problems away. Locking the door and collapsing in an office chair, Duke thought, "*How could this be happening?*" An hour ago, he was preparing to take a victory lap. He had a statement ready for the press. This was the first step of a promising political career. Inform the judge, and it's over. And if they ever discovered that he knew the DNA test was suspect, that would also end his career and probably send him to jail. They would ignore that Duke put a killer away and ensured he didn't rape and murder anyone else. They will hang him out to dry on a technicality. He had two DNA results and went with the one entered into evidence. Duke shook his head and thought, "*What else am I supposed to do? Baker, that poor excuse for a man, better keep his mouth shut.*"

Duke pushed himself up from his chair and paced

back and forth, stopping before his law diploma. The frame had a slight tilt. He straightened it, sat behind his desk, and found the judge's number in his contact book. He ran his finger over the number and tapped it several times.

The intercom buzzed, and his assistant said, "A network reporter wants to know if you have a few minutes for an interview. She is doing a story about young, powerful people on the rise."

Billings closed his contact book, straightened his tie, and said, "Send her in."

2) BAKER

Todd Baker trembled as he walked through Billings' outer office. He could feel the eyes upon him as one conversation after another trailed off, and heads turned to watch. There was near-total silence as he stood and waited for the elevator. An old-style clock clicked as each second passed. Above the elevator door, the red floor numbers slowly progressed. Each time they stopped, it seemed like an eternity, and Todd shifted his weight as he stared at the frozen digit, trying to will it onto the next floor. He thought, *"How long does it take for a person to get on an elevator? Come on, people, I need to get out of here."*

The staff was familiar with Baker's Walk of Shame. He was not the first to receive the 'Duke Billings' treatment. To be verbally undressed, bullied, and pushed to the point of breaking, then tossed unceremoniously from the office. During these episodes, you could not reason with the District Attorney; it was best to put your head down and weather the storm.

Billings' judgment became clouded, emotions ruled his decisions, and critical thinking took a backseat. His legal training became an afterthought, and his survival instincts kicked in. Billings did not believe in fight or flight; everything was fight.

A few staff members felt sorry for Baker, but most were glad it wasn't them. They didn't know what happened in Billings' office. But everyone knew not to mention it. Nobody wanted to be collateral damage. Keep your head down, do your job, and don't ask questions. That was the only way to survive if you worked for Billings.

The elevator opened, and people shuffled to the back, forming a small space in the front. Todd entered, tried to pull his shoulders tight, and turned back toward the office. Everyone's eyes darted back to their desk, pretending to work. In a packed elevator, Todd felt utterly alone as he descended to the garage.

Parked opposite Billings' black Mercedes Benz was Todd's small compact car. Billings' license plate read 'DA DUKE.' The 'DA' stood for District Attorney. Billings wanted it to read 'DUKE,' but a John Wayne fan beat him to it. He ran a police report on the man, hoping to find some leverage to force him to give him the plate. But the report came back clean. He placed a flag on the man's record; the police would report any activity to the District Attorney. Billings felt that the plate belonged to him. After all, he wasn't a fan of some long-dead movie star. He was Duke Billings.

The urge to run a key down the side of Billings' car came over Todd. He held it out and made a few pretend swipes, along with a scratching noise. Billings had no right to talk to him like that. He was doing his job, bringing critical information to the District Attorney. What's more important, a man's freedom or Billings' career? He could still smell Billings' breath. What was that tuna fish salad? Billings was right; Todd did screw up. But there was still time to correct the mistake. He had gone to Billings hoping for his help. Instead, he got a verbal lashing. Todd turned and got in his car. Scratching Billings' car wouldn't solve anything or make him feel better. Thinking about it was enough.

As Todd pulled out of the garage, his mind raced. The DNA report was wrong. Todd didn't do the test wrong; he messed up when comparing the result. Sample 66 was Jake Franklin, and sample 67 was from the crime scene. He compared sample 67 with sample 67. Of course, they matched.

Budget cuts had left the lab short-staffed. Todd was doing the work of three technicians, and Billings pressured him for a quick turnaround. That didn't excuse his mistake; it never should have happened. And when he got a 100% match, that should have sent up red flags. You never have a 100% match. The samples usually have some contamination, or the DNA degrades. But he was happy to have it done and off his desk.

He didn't think it through. It didn't register that the percentage match was extremely improbable. Typically, a second technician would verify the report. But no one else was at work, and Billings was demanding the results.

It was a short drive home. Hop on the interstate and head west. The sun was setting, and Todd lowered the shade to cut the glare and protect his eyes. His mind drifted, and he thought, "*What if the jury returns an innocent verdict? Then it would be no harm, no foul. Maybe Billings is right. The best course is to wait and see.*" The more Todd thought about it, the more convinced he became that this was the proper path. After all, he was acting on the advice of the District Attorney. He could go to the courtroom. If the verdict was guilty, he could stand and confess his mistake. Claim he had only discovered the error an hour ago. Billings wouldn't like it. But it would be done.

3) RESTLESS NIGHT

The jury had recessed without returning a verdict. Since deliberations started late in the day, this was not surprising. As a general rule, juries are quick to render a not-guilty verdict. Guilty verdicts require more time. The jury wants to seem thoughtful and thorough. Even if they have their mind made up, they will review each piece of evidence several times. After all, a man's freedom is at stake. It only seemed proper they devote most of a day discussing it. Also, one or two jurors usually want to be convinced. Sometimes it is because they enjoy being the center of attention, but usually, they do not want to take responsibility. It is easier to be on the losing side of an argument and claim no one would listen. Rather than stick your neck out and take a stand. Being on a jury does not negate human nature.

There are a small but significant number of cases where the jury can't decide. The judge usually orders them to keep trying, but at some point, he will declare it a hung jury. The prosecutor will then determine if they want to retry the case. This would be the best scenario for Billings. He could put off the decision on if to retry the case until the press lost interest. The American public was the only one with a shorter attention span than the media. However, this was highly unlikely. The judge was not about to let the jury off the hook. He would keep them deliberating until they decided. In the end, exhaustion will often do the work when reasoning fails.

Despite wanting to win the case, Duke secretly hoped for a hung jury or a not-guilty verdict. He would not receive the recognition he deserved, but at least the narrative wouldn't portray him as someone who mishandled the case. He could spin it as a fickle jury, unwilling to convict a predator. Claim that society had become soft on crime. It might even work toward his advantage. However, deep down, he was confident they would return a guilty verdict. He had presented a strong case, and the defense did a piss-poor job.

Of course, the defense attorney's poor performance is part of the reason there is a problem. Had he grilled Todd Baker on the DNA evidence, it would have been apparent that Baker didn't know shit. A different lab technician would have been assigned, and the question of which DNA test was correct would have been solved. Duke thought, "*The level of incompetents is staggering. They should fire both the defense attorney and the lab technician. The Halls of Justice are no place for those two baboons.*"

It was one a.m., and Duke had little chance of

falling asleep. He had gone to bed but could only stare at the ceiling. Reading didn't help. His eyes would scan the words, but his mind was elsewhere. He would read several pages and have no recollection of what was written. Too many thoughts were competing for his attention. He tossed and turned and stared into the darkness until he gave up and went and sat in his favorite chair. Scattered on the floor were several yellow legal pads with notes scribbled in black ink, only to be scratched out. An untouched bourbon was at his side. His mind turned over and over, reviewing the case.

The way the defense handled the DNA evidence was puzzling. If it was not Franklin's DNA, why wouldn't the defense have it tested by an independent lab? The only thing Duke came up with was that the victim was Franklin's assistant, and he was having an affair. They must have believed it was Franklin's DNA. He drove her home; they had sex, he left, and someone murdered her. But then, why didn't they testify he was banging her on the side? That would have explained the DNA and given reasonable doubt to the jury. And even if he wasn't having an affair and raped her, why wouldn't he lie and say he was having an affair? A rapist and murderer should have no problem adding liar to their list of character defects. Nothing made sense. It was maddening. Of course, the defense attorney was incompetent, so anything is possible. Duke thought, "*This is what happens when you dispense law degrees like candy.*"

Ultimately, the only thing that made sense was the defense team believed it was Franklin's DNA. They didn't want it retested because it would confirm the results. And Franklin was not having an affair. Otherwise, he would testify to the fact. The DNA must have resulted from him raping Suzy James. Baker's second test was the incorrect one.

None of this excused Duke's action. He was required to inform the judge. This was a judgment call he was not entitled to make. But at least he wasn't letting a rapist go free. His confidence grew that the second result was wrong and the first test was correct. The ends justify the means. Duke thought, "*Todd Baker needs to keep his mouth shut and do what he is told. The trouble with working with weak people is they panic. They can act unpredictably.*" Duke needed someone to watch Todd until the trial was over. He had to ensure Jake Franklin paid for his crime and didn't destroy his career.

Duke returned to bed, but his mind was still racing. He remembered that during most of the trial, Jake Franklin smirked, rolled his eyes, and made smart-ass comments to his lawyer. Whenever Duke looked at Franklin, he could see the contempt in his eyes. Duke was familiar with Franklin's kind—the pampered son of affluent parents, never facing life's hardships. Duke was looking forward to putting him away. Nobody was going to take that from him. Certainly not a little weasel like Baker.

He recalled coming from a poor family and working hard to earn a football scholarship. Then, his knee blew out in his junior year, and they took his scholarship. To finish school, he had to work two jobs. He would wait tables, serving people like Franklin. He remembered that same smirk as he served them their food. A technicality would not destroy his future. Franklin was guilty. He had to be; Billings' career depended on it.

4) JAKE

It was a cheap motel. On one side was the on-ramp to an interstate highway, and on the other was a 24-hour convenient store. Four of the five neon letters spelling 'MOTEL' were lit. The bed sagged in the middle, and the sheets were gray and thin from being washed an untold number of times. Mildew, urine, and disinfectant competed to be the dominant odor. In the drawer of the night table was a bible. The cover was stiff, and the pages pristine. People renting this room sought comfort from sources other than the Good Book.

Jake Franklin flipped through the channels on the television. One station sold a knife that could cut through a soda can and remained sharp enough to slice a tomato. It was only $19.95, and if you act now, you can get a set of steak knives for free. The next sold classic music albums with all the greatest hits, most of which Jake had listened to while growing up. They played ten-second clips of the songs. It seemed like a good deal, and you could make three easy payments. He stopped on a station where a preacher was healing people. "Do you believe?" the preacher asked. The person requesting help professed their belief. The preacher asked again, louder, looking into the audience. Encouraging them to declare their faith. It reached a fever pitch, with everyone in unison submitting to a higher power and confessing their belief. He laid his hands on the afflicted and told the devil to get out. And the person would walk, hear again, or no longer be an alcoholic. Healed, they raise their arms and dance around, thanking the lord and claiming a miracle had occurred.

That's what Jake needed, a miracle. If not a miracle, at least someone to believe him. His wife had kicked him out of their home and started divorce proceedings. She told him he was a cheater or a murderer, maybe both. She, like everyone else, believed the DNA results. Franklin knew they were incorrect. He had never had sex with Suzy, his assistant, whom he is charged with raping and murdering.

Suzy took care of the business end of the gym Jake owned. It was her twenty-third birthday. Jake and two of his employees took her out to celebrate. She drank too much, and Jake drove her home. He sat in his car and waited until she was safely inside her house. He then drove to his gym and spent two hours preparing for a self-defense class he was scheduled to teach the next day. The District Attorney used all of that against him.

Billings called it a convenient trip to the gym. Standing before the jury, making eye contact with several members, Duke said, "It is miraculous how this late-night workout accounts for the two hours between the time Franklin left the bar and got home. Home to his wife and four-year-old daughter. A daughter put to bed while her father was still out drinking." He ridiculed the idea that people go to the gym after a night of drinking. He suggested that the gym's showers were used to clean up blood. The defense attorney objected on grounds of speculation. The judge told the jury to disregard the last statement, but it was too late; the idea was firmly planted in the jury's mind. This and the DNA evidence were likely to get Jake convicted.

Jake had told his attorney the DNA needed to be retested. The attorney said he would look into it, but it never happened. Jake would have fired his attorney but didn't have money to hire a new one. He had given the attorney every cent he had. Sold the gym, cleaned out his savings, and would have taken out a second mortgage on the house, but his wife would not allow it. He spent every penny, and it was not enough. When Jake's funds ran out, and the attorney had to work on credit, he spent the minimum time possible on the case. Like everyone else, he saw where it was headed. He knew when Jake went to prison, he would never get paid. He would have dropped the case if the judge had allowed him.

The trial visibly annoyed Jake. He had expected to be cleared of any wrongdoing. As the trial proceeded, he could tell his attorney was no match for the District Attorney. His anger grew, and he would glare at the people giving testimony. The injustice infuriated him; he scowled at the judge, and the jury took notice. His attorney tried to coach him on how to act, but Jake would have none of it. He was innocent, and this whole proceeding and everyone involved offended him.

Suzy James had been his friend, and nobody was looking for her murderer. Against the advice of his attorney, he fully cooperated with the police. Jake urged, even begged, them to keep looking for the murderer. He repeated his story dozens of times to them. It never changed because it was the truth. But the police were determined to trip him up. They interrogated him for hours with no water or food. Trying to wear him down. They never considered he might be innocent. In most murder cases, the victim knows their attacker. That was enough for the police; as far as they were concerned, they had their man and looked no further than Jake Franklin.

Duke Billings was masterful. He painted a picture in the juror's mind of Jake murdering Suzy. He went over every detail of the murder scene. Describing Suzy's naked body lying spread eagle on the blood soak bed. Billings stood indignantly before the jury and said, "It wasn't enough to violate her. He also took his knife, held it to Suzy's neck, someone who had trusted him, an employee, a so-called friend, and slashed her throat. Then watched as the life drained from her eyes." Jake saw the jurors looking at him in disgust. The DNA evidence removed all doubt. The only problem, the DNA evidence was wrong, and Jake was the only one who believed it.

Tomorrow, he would sit in that courtroom and feel the hate radiating from the people surrounding him. Barring a miracle, he would be convicted of a crime he did not commit. And somewhere, a murderer was walking free, nobody searching for him.

5) THE VERDICT

It was a packed courtroom when Jake Franklin entered, followed by his lawyer. In the back row, a man wearing a pressed and starched shirt with a tie hopelessly out of date gave Jake a wide smile. He stopped short of waving, but it felt like he was. His clothes gave the appearance that he rarely attended public events, and this was the best his wardrobe offered.

Jake sat at the defendant's table and glanced back. "I've seen that man before," Jake said to his lawyer. "I just can't place him." His lawyer gave a half-hearted look and shrugged.

"On the night Suzy was killed, I think he may have been at the bar," Jake said. "Can you have someone check him out?"

"Let's focus on today. We can talk about that later," the lawyer said.

The parents of Suzy sat in the first row. They had been friends with Jake, and when the trial started, they believed Jake was not guilty. But as the trial progressed, Suzy's father's eyes hardened toward Jake. And her mother's head sunk lower with each passing day as her tears grew more frequent. Duke

Billings, aware of the parents, would pause after presenting a poignant piece of evidence, allowing the mother's sobs to fill the courtroom. A few jurors would dab their eyes, holding back tears.

Todd Baker was sitting about halfway back. He was squirming in his seat. His armpits created sweat stains on his shirt. Duke spotted him and nodded to a man sitting directly behind him. The man leaned forward, flashed a badge, and whispered, "I will arrest you immediately if you disrupt this courtroom." Todd turned pale and sank down into his seat.

Reporters filled most of the rest of the seats. A sketch artist sat in the first row and worked feverishly. With no cameras allowed, the evening news featured his drawings. They portrayed Duke Billings as strong and in control of the courtroom. While Jake Franklin's sketches showed him slumping in his seat, looking disrespectful.

The jury entered the courtroom in a single file, walking slowly, looking straight ahead. It was as if they were pole bearers without the casket. Everything in their body language signaled they would return a guilty verdict. As each entered the jury box, Duke attempted to make eye contact and give them an approving smile. The press would interview a few, and Duke wanted to ensure he left a favorable impression. A couple of them gave a knowing smile back and a slight nod.

A fleeting feeling of concern came over Duke. This was the last chance to halt the proceeding and let the judge know the DNA results were questionable. In a few minutes, it would be too late. A one-way threshold was about to be crossed. Duke took note that Franklin's wife was not present. He interpreted that as a sign Franklin was cheating on her and had committed the murder. Duke thought, *"Franklin is getting what he deserves. Justice is more important than a mere technicality."*

Franklin sat slouching at the defendant's table, scowling at the jury. His defense attorney tried to coach him on how to act, but Jake ignored his advice. Maybe he wasn't guilty, but he sure looked it. He was daring the jury to return a guilty verdict, and they were about to oblige.

Duke thought. *"It's not my fault they can't mount a proper defense. I am just doing my job. Doing what I'm hired to do, convince the jury to find Franklin guilty. Still, if the DNA evidence is questionable, is it right to sit by and let Franklin be convicted?"* Duke looked up at the judge. The judge gave a slight nod. *"That lab tech, what was his name? Todd Baker? Yeah, that was the little worm. Christ, doesn't anyone do their job? I wouldn't be in this mess if he knew how to do a simple DNA test. If this goes bad, he will say he told me, but that will look like he is trying to cover his ass. Just to be sure, I better tighten up that loose end. Maybe build a history of bad behavior. He deserves to be fired. Tonight's news story will not be that District*

Attorney Duke Billings screwed up a murder case and let a rapist get away. I'm sorry, but this is not my fault. That second DNA test is the one that is wrong."

"Has the jury reached a decision?" the judge asked. The courtroom grew quiet. Only the relentless drone of the air conditioner could be heard as it labored to provide relief to the stuffy room. Feet shuffled as people shifted in their seats. Suzy James' mother let out a sob that hung in the air. All eyes were cast toward the jury box.

The foreman stood, glanced at his fellow jurors, and said, "We have, Your Honor." He handed a folded-over paper to the bailiff. The bailiff accepted the verdict, solemnly walked over, and passed it to the judge.

People in the courtroom stirred as the judge opened the verdict. He gave a slight nod to the jury, cleared his throat, and said, "Jacob Franklin, you have been found guilty on all counts." An excited mummer rumbled through the crowd. The judge pounded his gavel until it died down. "Accordingly, I sentence you to life in prison without the possibility of parole. Sentence to begin immediately. Bailiff, take the prisoner into custody."

The reporters jumped out of their seats and headed for the door. Three or four trying to squeeze through at a time. The networks interrupted their regularly scheduled programs to bring breaking news. Camera crews stood by, waiting for their respected reporter to jump in front of the lens and report the verdict. The country was about to have a new hero and a new villain.

As Suzy's parents left the courtroom, the man sitting in the back row with the outdated tie expressed his sympathies. They thanked him for his kind thoughts. He held out his hand. Suzy's father took it with both hands, looked him in the eye, and with a sad smile, gave it a pat.

6) JAKE FRANKLIN

Two guards stepped forward and instructed Jake to put his hands behind his back. One guard handcuffed him and led him out the courtroom door. Photographers crowded the hallway, snapping pictures. They shouted, "Slimeball, rapist, coward, scum bucket," attempting to get Jake to give them an angry look. It wasn't anything personal; it just made for a better picture. The TV stations would promote their six o'clock news with a photo of Jake, fiery eyes, neck bulging, and the word CONVICTED diagonally stamped across the picture. The voice-over would say, "Murderer, off the streets, details at six."

Jake Franklin, now convicted of murder, was taken to a small conference room in the back of the courthouse. It was cramped and smelled of musty papers. A small window air conditioning unit struggled but only spewed out warm air. A guard put his hand on Jake's shoulder and forced him to sit on an old wooden chair. The table before him contained deep scars where hundreds of prisoners had dragged handcuffs across its surface. Someone had scratched the word 'Justice' with a circle surrounding it and a slash across it.

Adam Hall, Jake's attorney, sat across from him. He held his briefcase in his lap and did not make eye contact. "The DNA evidence was too damning. Are you going to be, Okay?" Adam pulled at his tie and glanced toward the door. He had a tired, defeated look in his eyes. The same look Jake had seen for weeks.

"I'll be okay when you get me out of here. That was not my DNA. Why were you unable to show that?" Jake shifted forward and slammed his cuffed hands down on the table. The guard straightened up and put his hand on his sidearm.

"I did what I could. I had experts explain how DNA can be mistaken. The jury didn't buy it. There was too much evidence against you. And you didn't help. You should've come clean."

"Clean about what?" Jake pushed forward and stared at Adam.

"Your DNA came from somewhere. I don't care what two consulting adults do in private. And I know it would have ended your marriage, which is happening away, but telling the jury you had an affair with your assistant would have explained the DNA. It would have given you a chance."

"How many times do I have to tell you? I wasn't having an affair. We never had sex. It wasn't my DNA." Jake leaned back in his chair. "I want a new DNA test. An independent lab, like I told you before. You can't ask the same person to do the same test. Of course, they will get the same results. We need to file an appeal as soon as possible. Also, have someone investigate that guy who was sitting in the back row. I think he was at the bar. He may know something. Hell, he may be the actual murderer."

"You can't afford an independent test. Or an investigator. But I'll leave that up to whichever lawyer handles your appeal." Adam pulled his briefcase closer to his chest and turned his chair toward the door.

"What do you mean, whichever lawyer? I want you to file an appeal. And do it right away."

"Jake, you already owe me more than you can ever pay. I can't do this pro bono. I worked the last few months without pay because walking out wouldn't be right. But unless you have some money hidden away. This is where we part company."

Jake leaned forward and slammed his arms on the table. The guard took a step and glared at Jake. "I've given you everything I have. I mortgaged my house and sold my car. Everything. I'm an innocent man. This should not have gone to trial. I gave my assistant, who had too much to drink, a ride home. A woman I have worked with for five years, someone who has been to my house, met my wife and played with my daughter. Someone I care about. I didn't want her driving drunk, and that is enough evidence to convict me of murder?"

"The DNA, Jake. The DNA."

"It is not mine. Have someone not connected with the case retest it. Someone who doesn't have to cover their ass because they made a mistake. Someone who is not in the District Attorney's pocket."

"Sorry, Jake. I have bills like everyone else. I can't work for free. Too bad you didn't get the death penalty; plenty of lawyers would be willing to file pro bono appeals." Adam regretted making that statement. He shook his head and shrugged his shoulders. "They have a law library. You'll have to do most of the work yourself. You're part of the system now. Convicted of raping and murdering your assistant, no one will touch you. Sorry to be blunt." Adam stood. "I have to focus on my other clients. I need to bring in some money and pay some bills."

"Get out," Jake said. "You know the murderer is still out there. No one is looking for him. He will probably murder again. That is on you, and on that pretentious District Attorney, and on whoever can't do a simple DNA test."

Adam Hall headed for the door. He turned around and said, "Sorry, Jake. I did the best I could with what you gave me."

"Do you believe I'm innocent?" Jake stared at his attorney. "Did you ever believe I was innocent?

Were you in my corner? Were you fighting for me with everything you had? As if my life depended on it. Because it does?"

"I wanted to believe. But it's hard to argue with DNA. You didn't listen to me, Jake. Admitting to an affair is better than being convicted of murder."

"No shit. The problem is, I didn't have an affair. I've never cheated on my wife. And I did not rape and murder Suzy James. Christ, I've never even had a parking ticket."

"Time to go," the guard said. He grabbed Jake by the elbow and forced him to stand.

"Do you believe me?" asked Jake. "I need someone to believe me."

"Sure, if that makes you feel better. Everyone I take to prison is innocent. Why not you?"

"Listen, a guy was sitting in the last row. He had a big smile and was wearing an outdated tie. Can you check him out? Something is not right with him."

"Sorry, not my job."

"You work for the Justice Department. Justice, it's part of your title. How can it not be your job?"

"My job is to take your sorry ass to prison. Let's go."

7) LAST CALL

It was a corner bar, the type that had a small but loyal clientele. At noon, a few regulars would wander in and chat with the bartender as she refilled drink mixes, cut garnishes, and wiped down the surface areas. They would do some harmless flirting, and she would smile and engage in verbal jousting. She was well-versed in making them feel welcome while letting them know where the boundaries were. As the day wore on, others entered the bar, and the initial patrons faded into the background. Slumping on their barstools and hugging their beer. They would stagger out at some point, turning the bar over to the night crowd.

Stan was not a regular. But he liked this type of bar. He blended in and became almost invisible. No one saw him, and no one remembered him being there. He was interchangeable with the multitude of middle-aged men whose daily routine took them from work, to a barstool, to a recliner.

A special report came on the news, and Stan waved, attempting to get the bartender's attention. "Turn up the volume. I want to hear this," he shouted. The bartender stopped washing glasses, picked up a remote, and slightly increased the volume. Stan motioned with his thumb to turn it louder. The bartender raised it one more notch, put the remote down, and walked away.

Duke Billings, dressed in a dark blue suit and red tie, was reading a prepared statement to the press. "Today, we made the streets safer. We put away a rapist and murderer. Jake Franklin will never prey on the innocent women of the Great State of Ohio again."

Hands shot up from all the reporters, and Duke pointed at one. "Franklin claims it was not his DNA."

"We have very skilled lab technicians. They testified to the results, and the defense cross-examined. I refer you to their expert testimony," Duke said.

"Franklin claims you have a personal vendetta against him."

"I do not know Jake Franklin. I only know of his horrendous deeds. I follow the evidence, regardless of the defendant. Justice is blind."

Stan slapped the bar and laughed. He turned to an old man sitting beside him, nursing a beer. "Did you hear that? Justice is blind. He got that right."

The old man, who was as much a fixture as the jukebox or the neon beer signs, wiped beer suds from his lips and said, "They should have given him the death penalty. Only a no-good coward would rape and murder a drunk girl. A man like that is worse than vermin who crawl through the sewers."

"Shut up, old man. What the hell do you know?" Stan turned to the TV and watched the reporters jockey for position. The questions were all the same, but neither Billings nor the reporters cared. It was about getting face time on the tube. And you never knew when a clip would hit a cord and go viral.

Someone put money in the jukebox, the TV sound cut off, and the music played. It was better watching it without the volume. Duke stood tall and straight behind a podium, several feet above the reporters. They strained their necks, looking up at him like a pack of dogs waiting for a treat. He would point, and you could imagine the reporter's tail wagging.

The old man was stewing, feeling disrespected. He turned toward Stan. "Listen, I know a lot more than you. You're nothing more than a punk. You need to learn some respect."

A young female entered the bar and saw her grandfather arguing with Stan. She put her hand on the old man's back. "Come on, gramps. It's time to go home."

Stan glanced at the female. She had a slight build

with long brown hair. He could smell her perfume. It had a faint vanilla scent. "You need help with him?" Stan asked.

She smiled at Stan. "No. I hope he wasn't bothering you?" The young lady turned to her grandfather, who was trying to delay his departure. She helped him figure out his tab. Tried to add a few extra dollars to the tip, but her grandfather made her take it back.

"Nah, just having a little fun. Right old man?"

"You're still a punk," the old man said. He got up slowly, letting his granddaughter hold him by the elbow.

The granddaughter gave Stan a nervous laugh, and Stan smiled back. "Don't worry about it. It's all good. We were having a friendly argument. Sure, you don't need a hand?"

"No, I've done this many times. Since my grandmother passed away, he has spent his time here. I guess he can't stand being alone in his house. Come on, gramps, watch your step."

The two of them made their way to the door. Stan thought, "*No more. I got away with the last one. Quit while you're ahead. That's what they say. She is a cute little thing. A bit of a tease. Smiling at me. Wearing that skirt with those long legs. You think her parents would have taught her better. Nope, I'm done with it. That grandfather is a real piece of work. He called me a punk. It would serve him right if I tied him up and made him watch. No. No. No. I'm not doing it again. I'm not pressing my luck. It was a one-time deal, and I got away with it. Although I doubt the District Attorney could catch me."*

Stan tossed the money for his drinks on the bar, went to the door, and watched as she helped her grandfather into her car. He got into his beat-up Ford Ranger and followed her to a small one-story house in an older neighborhood. Overgrown maple trees lined the streets. The sidewalks were cracked and uneven. There were a few abandoned houses and some empty lots where homes had been torn down. This once middle-class working neighborhood was long past its prime. And the houses, like the people that inhabited them, were waiting for their time to expire. Stan thought, *"Have the decency to bury the dead."*

Parking on a side street, he watched the young girl fumbling with the front door keys while trying to keep her grandfather from falling down the steps. The house lights lit up, first the living room, then the kitchen, then the back bedroom. It was a welcoming sight, with the warm yellow light spilling out of the windows. The front door remained partly open, and the keys hung from the lock.

Stan pulled out his knife. He ran his finger over the edge, testing its sharpness. Talking to himself, Stan said, "Maybe I won't have to kill her. I'll explain; I saw the door open and wanted to make sure she was all right. She will offer me a drink, and we can talk. Maybe become my girlfriend. That would be a hoot. That old man and I can watch football games and have good-natured arguments. She will cook us dinner and bring me a beer. Kiss me on the cheek and tell me not to get him excited. I hope she is nice."

Stan silently slid into the house, took the keys, and locked the door. Voices came from the back bedroom as she put her grandfather to bed. Stan picked up a dish towel and pulled out his knife. He stood flat against the wall, waiting. His heart was pounding. He caught a faint whiff of her perfume; it had a pleasant fresh smell. *I need to make sure she doesn't scream. Just need time to explain. I hope she's not like the last girl. Maybe we can be friends,"* he thought.

She stepped to the door, turned back, and whispered, "Goodnight" to her grandfather. When she turned back, Stan placed the towel over her mouth and nose and put the knife to her throat.

At that same moment, District Attorney Duke Billings smiled as he drank bourbon and watched news clips of his press conference. Meanwhile, Jake Franklin was spending his first night in prison as a convicted murderer.

8) PRISON

Jake Franklin spent the time between his arrest and conviction working out. Increasing his stamina and fitness, practicing new self-defense tactics, and learning different ways to kill a man. He was determined not to be victimized.

Before selling it for legal expenses, Jake owned a gym and was already in top shape. He was also an expert at Jujutsu and several other martial arts. He had spent his entire life teaching others how to defend themselves, and now those skills were all he had left. His first rule was to keep his head down and stay to himself. His second rule was to act without hesitation and with maximum force.

Jake was entering a world of hard men. Many have been in this environment all their adult life. He felt his only course was to show no weakness and fight if he had to, most likely to the death, his death. But with the State having taken his freedom, if required, he will trade his life for some measure of dignity. Of course, this is probably what most men say when entering prison. But until they face the ferocity of the beast, feel its hot breath on their neck, and stare into the abyss of its dark black eyes, they do not know how you will react.

A guard escorted Jake down a lengthy stretch of cells. The stench of urine and sweat permeated from the concrete walls, while the fluorescent bulbs, covered in layers of dust, emitted a dim and artificial light. The clamor of countless men, restlessly pacing, tossing on rigid bunks, coughing, and shouting crude remarks, reverberated throughout the corridors. It all blended into the unsettling atmosphere of a manmade jungle, transforming the hearts of men into those of beasts. Confined within those cells, the inmates were not being rehabilitated, destined to reenter society; they were adapting and evolving to survive this harsh, unnatural, unholy reality.

The guard stopped midway down the row of cells, placed his key in the lock, and the heavy metal door clanked and groaned as it opened. An older man was lying on the lower bunk. He did not look up or acknowledge Jake as he entered the cell. The guard signaled, and the door slid shut. Life without the possibility of parole had begun.

Settling into the top bunk, Jake stared at the ceiling. It had only been a day since the trial ended, but time was playing tricks. His old life, the people he knew, the places he went, and the things he cared about all seemed in the distant past. He tried and failed to recall the faces of friends and family; his mind went blank. His only images were of guards putting handcuffs on him, pushing him through doors, and making him stand naked as they searched for contraband. Talking to each other, the guards ignored Jake, only occasionally barking an order, referring to him as inmate, stripping away his personal identity as they had stripped away his clothes.

He was in prison, and he realized for the first time he had nothing to do. No schedule to keep, no chores to complete, and nobody depending on him. It would be that way tomorrow, the next day, and every day after that, for the rest of his life. Not only had they deprived him of his freedom, but they had also taken his sense of purpose.

It was over an hour before his cellmate spoke. "Did you do it?" Came the question from the lower bunk.

"The jury said I did."

"Not what I asked."

"No. I didn't," said Jake. He had given considerable thought to how he would answer that question. If he claimed to be a murderer, would that give him some cred? Maybe people would leave him alone. But then, he would also be admitting he was a rapist. In the end, he decided the hell with them. He would never accept the verdict and do everything possible to get it overturned.

"I did," said his cellmate. "Twenty-three years ago. In cold blood. He had already given me the money out of the cash register. No reason to shoot him. But I saw him shaking, fear in his eyes, and figured I should put him out of his misery. I've read books on the subject. Some claim I was shooting myself. I felt fear and hated myself for it. This young man, a boy really, I projected myself onto him. I killed him, hoping to kill my fear. What do you think of that theory?"

"Sounds like bullshit to me," Jake said.

"Yeah. That's what I think too. The simple answer is I just wanted to shoot him. His fear was over the top, too extreme. He ended up cowering in a corner. I get it. If someone points a gun at you, you'll tremble, maybe stutter; it's only natural. But he wet his pants. I've only seen that in movies. In real life, it is ten times worse. He was shaking so hard that I thought he would have a heart attack. His eyes were wide open, and his hands were trying to cover his head as if that would do any good. It was an awful sight. That's no way to live your life. So I ended it for him."

The cellmate tossed in his bunk and said, "I have no remorse, never have. They say it is because I'm a psychopath." The cell was quiet for a few minutes. "Don't let that worry you. Five percent of the population are psychopaths. It's rare for us to kill anyone. Just don't piss on the toilet seat. I hate that."

"If I do, I'll clean it up."

"That's all I ask." The cellmate turned toward the wall. "I'm Ben. Do you have remorse?"

"I'm Jake. And like I said. I didn't do it."

"That's what I used to say. It makes no difference," Ben said. "If you snore, it's best you don't go to sleep. It's not as bad as pissing on the seat. But it still bothers me."

Jake lay in his bunk, wide awake, not because of what Ben said, but because his mind was racing. His attorney made it clear he would not handle his appeal and that Jake still owed him fifty thousand dollars. His wife was divorcing him and told him not to expect any visits from her or his four-year-old daughter. And his cellmate was a psychopath and had already threatened him twice.

How did they get the DNA wrong? He had to find a way to retest it, but not by the State. Jake had observed the District Attorney's press conference. He saw him flinch when the reporter mentioned that the case was based solely on DNA evidence. The District Attorney, Duke Billings, knows something is wrong with that test.

9) HIGHER OFFICE

At four feet ten inches, Clay Mason was short but stocky. He wore expensive tailored suits and walked slowly, accustomed to people waiting for him. Duke stood near a coffee table in the corner of his office, ready to greet him. A man of Mason's caliber, you didn't sit behind a desk.

Duke had a forced smile as he waited to shake the man's hand. He had met Mason twice before, and while cordial, the meetings left him slightly uneasy. Mason spoke in riddles, never saying what he meant, always leaving it open for interpretation. It had the feeling of doing something wrong, something slightly sleazy. As if they were boys hiding behind the garage looking at nudie magazines while their mother stared out the kitchen window, trying to see what they were up to.

Duke gave Mason a firm handshake and offered him a seat in front of a polished cherry coffee table. At the center of the table was an Ohio State football helmet. Reminding everyone, Duke was a minor football celebrity. The NFL would have drafted him if not for a career-ending knee injury.

"I used to watch you play," Mason said. "Always figured I would see you in a Bengals jersey."

Duke rubbed his knee and shrugged. "Sometimes fate has other ideas."

"Yeah, that injury was heartbreaking. I was in the stadium. Never heard fifty thousand people so quiet."

"We move on. Besides, it would have been a Browns jersey," Duke said.

Mason, a kingmaker in Ohio politics, was here to offer his support should Duke run for Attorney General. All the big donors waited for Mason's seal of approval. He also controls a considerable amount of the press. You could run without his support, but good luck winning.

Mason didn't care about political issues. He only cared about political power. He was here to ensure Duke knew how to repay favors and keep secrets. As far as the issues were concerned, you said what your political base expected. It was the same script for you and everyone else in the party. All you needed to do was repeat the same dozen short, vague statements, and the voters would hear what they wanted. If you were out to change the world, to save mankind from himself, you were in the wrong business.

Duke had chosen the District Attorney's office over a lucrative private practice as a pathway to higher office. He had nothing against money. In fact, he liked it; the more, the better. But it was the power he craved. At night, sitting alone with his bourbon, he would let his mind wander. He would see himself as a Senator or the Governor, and if he let it wander long enough, he would be sitting in the Oval Office. But part of the dance was to play coy. To do the whole 'Who? Little old me?' routine. So, he waited for Mason to make the first move.

"As you know, the current Attorney General is from the other party," said Mason. He clasped his hands together and pretended to be deep in thought. "We think he is vulnerable. A young law and order type like yourself would have a real shot at unseating him."

"I'm pretty busy with my current job. I've promised my district to make the streets safe. There is still a lot of work to be done." Duke leaned back in his chair, smiled, and nodded.

"And doing a fine job. Putting Jake Franklin away, well, that was first-rate work. A lot of people took notice. A lot of important people."

"The jury is the one who found him guilty. I just set the table."

"The party would fully support your run. Of course, you would have to do some fundraising. But the party can introduce you to some influential donors." With his hands still clasped, Mason leaned forward, extended his index fingers, and pointed them at Duke. "It's never too early to build a donor base. It can come in handy if later you seek an even higher office. You never know."

Duke walked over to his bookcase and took a football off the shelf. He tossed it a few inches in the air and caught it. He had practiced this move many times. Showing he was part of the team without saying it. It was hokey, but effective.

"What are Roger Armstrong's chances? Is he going to be the next governor?"

"Up by ten points. And he is a big fan of yours. You can count on a few joint appearances." Mason motioned for Duke to toss him the football. "We have a strong team. You would make an excellent addition. And think how much more you can do as Attorney General."

The conversation continued like a poorly scripted B movie. They both knew that Duke would run, and this was just a formality. Nothing more than foreplay, but everyone likes to be kissed first.

"Well, you have given me a lot to think about," Duke said, putting the football back on the shelf.

"Don't take too long. A lot of powerful people are lining up to give you their support." Mason shook Duke's hand again and opened the door. He turned around and said, "I saw the paper this morning. Another rape and murder. Make sure you stop him like you did the last one. Knock them down, one scumbag at a time. Hey, maybe that can be your campaign slogan. Nah, probably not."

Duke walked over to his desk. He opened the bottom drawer and pulled out an old pay stub. It was from a greasy spoon restaurant in a small town. At fourteen, he worked as a dishwasher. The stub showed they paid him $32 for twenty hours of work, four of which went to taxes.

He remembers working in that hot kitchen all summer while his friends were out playing. He swore he would make it out of that small town, a town that was in decline, as one by one, the surrounding factories closed.

"Attorney General," Duke smiled. "And I'm not done yet."

10) TODD BAKER

Todd tossed the DNA test results onto the lab table. He had checked and rechecked the results. He even rechecked the results from the Jake Franklin case. Without a doubt, the DNA matched in both incidents. The person who committed this latest rape and murder also perpetrated the crime for which Jake Franklin was serving a life sentence.

He had told District Attorney Duke Billings that he had mixed up the samples in the initial case. But the District Attorney had convinced him to stay quiet. Todd looked at his phone. He had called the District Attorney three times, with no answer and no return call. He wanted to text, but the District Attorney warned him against texting or voice messages. Todd had made one mistake, two if you want to count relying on Duke Billings. Now the situation was spiraling out of control. It wouldn't be long before someone found out what he did. Who knows, they may already be on to him.

A technician entered the lab. She logged into her computer and entered some data. A few drops of sweat rolled down Todd's forehead. Her name was Samantha, Sam for short. She was a recent hire.

Todd thought, *"What's she doing here? Is she spying on me? Do they know I doctored the DNA results?"*

"Are you all right?" Sam asked.

"Me. Yes. Why?"

"You're pale. You look like you're going to faint."

"I had a late night. Not as young as I used to be," Todd said. "Why are you here? I mean, what are you working on?"

"Blood analysis. A man's dog went missing. The next day there is blood smeared on his door," Sam said. "But it turns out it's cow's blood. Most likely got it from a butcher. Hopefully, the pooch is alright. Maybe a prank. People are sick." Sam walked over to Todd's workstation. "How about you? Anything interesting?"

Todd shoved the DNA results inside a folder. "That rape and murder from the other day."

"Oh, that was awful," Sam said. "You know, it reminds me of the Jake Franklin case. If he wasn't in prison, I would think we had a serial killer on our hands."

"No, definitely different," Todd said.

"Maybe a copycat. I better let you get back to work. You don't want to be responsible for letting a murderer go free."

Waiting until Sam left, Todd locked up the test results and glanced at his watch. It was 4:30 pm.

"Billings is responsible for this," Todd thought. *"He told me not to come forward with the correct DNA. I'm an employee. I do what the District Attorney tells me. Now we have a serial killer loose and an innocent man in prison. Billings can spin this any way he wants, but he did it, not me."*

Todd got in his car and drove to the District Attorney's office. The parking garage was only half full, with many employees leaving for the day. But the District Attorney's black Mercedes was parked in his reserved space. Todd backed into the parking space beside him, lining up the driver-side windows. If he didn't want to talk on the phone, they could have a conversation here.

On the radio was a news report on the recent murder. A police lieutenant said they had no leads and asked anyone with information to come forward. Turning off the radio, Todd slid back in his seat, waiting for Billings to appear. His stomach was aching, and his head was throbbing. He closed his eyes. If only he could sleep, but it was impossible.

It was close to seven o'clock before the District Attorney appeared. By that time, the garage was almost empty. Billings strolled across the parking lot, his head down, reading from his phone. He did not notice Todd and opened his car door.

Todd rolled down his window and said, "I tried to call you three times."

Billings, startled, dropped his keys. He then frowned at Todd, got in his car, and rolled the window down. "I told you never to contact me. This better be good."

"We have a big problem. That rape and murder from yesterday."

"What rape and murder?"

"You're the District Attorney. Christ, check the news. Some creep follows a woman home from a bar, rapes, and murders her and her grandfather."

Billings started his car and turned the radio on. "Turn your radio on. Not too loud, just enough to create some white noise. So why are you telling me this?"

"Does any of this sound familiar?"

"So what? It happens all the time. This is a big city."

"So what? The DNA is the same as from the Jake Franklin case." Todd realized he was talking too loud and lowered his voice. "It's the same guy. He has murdered another woman."

Duke Billings paused momentarily, gazing through the windshield of his car at the grimy concrete garage wall from which paint chips were flaking away. The scent of exhaust fumes filled the air, and somewhere in the distance, he heard the squeaking tires of a car as it maneuvered around the sharp turns.

"What should I do?" asked Baker.

"Why are you asking me?" Duke slammed his fist on the steering wheel.

"You got us into this. Told me not to report my mistake."

"I did not. You came to me begging for me to save your job. I didn't do anything. You're the one who screwed up. You were giving me test results left and right. I didn't know what to believe. So, I went with what you testified, under oath, in a court of law. Now I have to save your ass again?"

"If I enter the latest results, they will know the initial one is wrong. You put Jake Franklin in prison. There is no way he committed this murder."

"A jury of his peers convicted him in a fair trial. I only presented the evidence that you provided me. If this goes south, it's on you, not me."

"What should I do?"

"I don't know. Contaminate the DNA sample. Say it came that way. Tell them it is useless and you need another one. It will be too late to get a new sample."

"What about Franklin?"

"What about him?"

"He is innocent."

"We don't know that. I present the evidence I had at the time. A jury convicted Franklin. It is up to his lawyer to appeal. I can't save both your ass and his. Now don't phone me again. If you must talk to me, do it like this. Meet me in the garage."

"What about the serial killer? This DNA may help catch him."

"I don't trust any of your results. You've screwed up before. You probably screwed this up. The police will do fine without your help. Do what I say, and stay away from me."

Duke threw his car in gear, leaving Todd alone in the garage.

11) SHOWER

It was shortly after dinnertime on Jake Franklin's third day of incarceration. He had not showered yet, but knew it could not be avoided. He picked up a small bar of soap and his towel.

Ben, his cellmate, was in his bunk reading a three-year-old Field and Stream magazine from the prison library. He glanced at Jake and said, "It's about time. The fellows are getting impatient."

"What's that supposed to mean?" Jake stood in front of Ben, looking down at him.

Ben laid his magazine on his chest. "You're a rapist. And some of the fellows have a bit of a vigilante streak."

"Is that a threat?" Jake glared at Ben.

"You're confusing a threat for a warning. Me, I couldn't care less. I have no part in this. But a few of the boys feel they are doing the lord's work. You know, an eye for an eye. There is a lot of talk about that poor girl you raped."

"Are you saying I'm going to be raped?"

"My advice is don't fight it. They get off on the struggle. The more you fight, the better they like it. So just go limp and take it. That will take the fun out of it, and they will leave you alone in the future."

"Are you talking from experience?"

"Me, hell no. I'm no rapist. Just your everyday murderer. But you, that was just sick what you did to that girl. And her being drunk and helpless, some of the fellows think you have it coming to you."

"I told you I'm innocent."

"Now you are being downright disrespectful of the American judicial system. People went through a lot of trouble to ensure you got a fair trial. Twelve jurors, your peers, all think you did it. Now all twelve can't be wrong. And that District Attorney who convicted you. He seems like a fine man. Why I heard talk, he will be running for Attorney General. What is his name, Duke Billings? That even sounds like someone you can trust."

"What about the guards?" Jake stepped outside the cell and looked in both directions.

"The guards, there are only a few of them and over a hundred of us. They don't go anywhere near the shower. A lot of perverted stuff happens in there. They don't want to get involved. Let the inmates sort it out. That's their motto. Besides, most agree with the fellows that you have it coming. The guards will be busy elsewhere. There is one that likes to watch. A real pervert, that one. He may be around, but he ain't going to help."

"I'm not going to let it happen." Jake paced back and forth in his cell, looking for anything he could use to defend himself. "If anyone touches me, they will be sorry."

"That's the spirit. The fellows are going to have fun with you." Ben sat up and looked at Jake. "What I heard is there is only going to be one. His name is Bruce, and he is a big sucker. He paid a pack of cigarettes to get to do you alone. No way you can take him. As I said, best to go limp. He may lose interest and just beat the crap out of you."

"I don't care how big he is."

"If you fight him, he is going to get aroused. Then it's best to pretend you're getting a prostate exam. When you think about it, what's the difference? You bend over for your doctor." Ben chuckled, then looked Jake in the eyes. "After it's over, go to Rupert. He runs the Aryans. Tell him you understand it had to be done, and you want to keep your head down and do your time. Most likely, they will leave you alone."

"Like hell, I will."

"You keep talking like you have a choice. You keep thinking you control what happens to you. If you controlled things, would you be here in the first place?" Ben watched as Jake paced. "I like you, Jake. You don't snore. You don't make a mess. I actually believe you are innocent. Not that it matters.

Even if Bruce knew you were innocent, he would convince himself you weren't. This little bit of vigilante justice is something the boys can believe in, giving them a tiny bit of purpose. They aren't about to let the truth get in the way. Besides, Bruce just enjoys it."

12) BRUCE

Jake proceeded down the corridor. The lockdown was over an hour away, and most cells remained open. The energy in the cellblock was different. There was a feeling of anticipation. Inmates stared and whispered to each other as Jake walked past. A few made a kissing sound. Jake ignored them and stared straight ahead. This would be his first shower since being incarcerated. And while he would have liked to put it off, he knew delaying would signal fear.

Jake's cellmate Ben warned him that Bruce was waiting to administer vigilante justice. Those convicted of rape were targets for similar treatment. The prisoners didn't have a moral compass that made them believe in an eye for an eye. Rather, it was a convenient excuse to intimidate and coerce inmates. It also broke up the boredom. Even the inmates that didn't take part, which was most of them, had something to talk about. And some, like Bruce, a beast of a man, seemed to enjoy administering it more than most. The guards turned a blind eye, believing the rapist were getting what they deserved.

The shower was a large, open room. One side had lockers to store your towel and clothes, with a row of rough wooden benches, the green paint worn thin. Shower heads lined the opposite side. The tile walls were old, and the grout was dark and stained from mold. They assigned inmates to keep the showers clean, and the inmates did the job as well as you could expect from someone who didn't give a shit.

Two inmates stood at the door and smiled as Franklin entered. Only one person was taking a shower, a skinny middle-aged man, not Bruce. Jake put his clothes in a locker and took a small plastic bag containing a bar of soap and a clear liquid. He took a whiff of the liquid and jerked his head back. He turned on the shower and held his hand in the spray, hoping it would warm up. Hot water, privacy, and security were in short supply.

"Come on, slim. You're clean. Get out of here," the inmate at the door said. The skinny man grabbed his stuff and rushed from the room.

Jake wiped the showerhead next to him clean. It provided a reflective surface, enabling him to see the door. Not enough for a clear image, but enough to know if anyone was approaching from behind. He opened his plastic bag, taking out the soap, being careful not to spill the liquid.

It didn't take long for a big, hairy man to enter the room. Tattoos ran the length of his arms, and stenciled across his chest was a Nazi Swastika. Halfway across, he stopped and scratched himself. The man had several teeth missing and a large scar over his right eye.

"You're that rapist," Bruce said.

"I don't want any trouble. I'm just doing my time," Jake said.

"I heard you claim you didn't do it."

"You heard right." Jake continued to shower, keeping an eye on the reflection in the shower head.

"I didn't do any of the stuff I did either. I'm a pillar of the community." Bruce laughed at his joke and looked back at the two inmates guarding the door. They gave a half laugh and a forced smile in a show of support.

"I'm just doing my time. Nothing else concerns me." Outside the gym, Jake had never been in a street fight. But he had fought plenty of men inside a ring. He usually won his fights, but inside the ring, there were rules and a referee. This fight would not have rules, and nobody would stop it if it got out of control.

Bruce was big, but Jake had practiced taking larger men down. If you didn't have the advantage of strength, use leverage and speed. Jake had another advantage. For Bruce, this was another victim, one more person to brutalize. For Jake, it was life or death. If he let this happen, others would try the same thing. Bruce did not intend to kill him, but what type of life would he have left? No, this had to be a life-or-death fight.

"I bet that girl was real scared when you raped her. You get off on that, scaring little girls. The way I see it, you need to pay for that. You need to know what it feels like." Bruce put his arm around Jake's neck and leaned in. "Me and you are going to have a little fun. I bet that girl begged you to stop. Well, I'm not going to stop either."

Jake reached into the plastic bag and threw the liquid in Bruce's eyes. Bruce screamed in pain and released Jake. His hands automatically rubbed his eyes, making it worse. The smell of bleach filled the air. Jake pivoted, lowered his shoulder, and flew into Bruce's midsection, driving him into the wall. Bruce's head bounced off the wall and dazed him. Jake threw a forearm at Bruce's jaw, crashing his head back into the wall. Bruce collapsed, unconscious, making a loud thud as he hit the floor.

Jake grabbed Bruce's head by the hair, ready to beat it against the floor. But he hesitated. He thought to himself, "*Don't leave a wounded animal. Finish him.*" But he couldn't do it. He knew to end this, he had to kill Bruce. But he wasn't there yet. They had convicted him, branded him as a killer, a murderer. But he wasn't a killer, not yet, anyway.

He glanced at the two inmates standing at the door, mouths open. They took several steps back, turned, and ran. Jake was alone, standing over a bleeding, bruised mound of flesh. A predator who had brought nothing but pain and suffering to the world. If Bruce was a hungry wolf killing livestock to survive, Jake would have no problem shooting it. So why can't he kill this animal, an animal that can think and reason and has no cause to attack others? An animal that inflicts pain for the joy of it. It wasn't his morals that prevented him from killing Bruce. It was his training, his programming, thou shall not kill.

As Jake returned to his cell, a wave of whispering proceeded him down the corridor. This time, the inmates stood in shocked silence or turned away as he passed. A few had a faint smile. Three inmates ran toward the shower. They stopped and stepped aside, standing flat against the wall, trying to make themselves as small as possible as Jake passed them.

13) BEN

Ben, Jake's cellmate, lay on his bunk reading a steamy romance novel. The prison library depends on donated books, and a significant number of them are romance novels. In a prison filled with murderers, thieves, and drug pushers, there are a surprisingly large number of fans of this genre. The steamier parts have the corner of their pages turned down; most inmates only read those parts.

At one time, a nun ran a prison reading program. She tried to get them to read Macbeth, but the inmates insisted on reading erotic passages to her. She lasted less than three weeks.

"I thought you only read philosophy books," Jake said.

"It's important to read a wide range," said Ben. "Besides, nothing wrong with a little entertainment. What surprises me is most of these are by female authors. There is a lot of pent-up sexual energy out there. Women looking for strong, healthy men. Men with an appetite. What a waste that I'm stuck inside. I could be a real asset to society. I'm going to bring it up at my next parole hearing."

Ben had read almost all the books in the library. He was probably the most well-read, intelligent person Jake knew. He had even written and published a book. It sold extremely well, with all the proceeds going to his victim's family. He wrote a second book and requested a few dollars for his commissary account. When the victim's family refused, he burned the book. Jake wondered what Ben could have made of his life if he hadn't killed that person. When he asked Ben that question, Ben shrugged.

"I suppose you think you accomplished something. You think the beating you gave Bruce ends things?" Ben said.

"I did what I had to," Jake said. Jake glanced down the prison hallway. A few inmates were standing by the railings, deep in conversation. One looked up, smiled, and pretended to be boxing.

"That's just it. You didn't." Ben tossed the book on the floor. "Why didn't you finish the job? Why didn't you kill him?" Ben shook his head.

"It's not a simple thing to do. Kill a man, even if he deserves it."

"You are in here because you killed and raped a woman. What, you only kill women?"

"I told you; I didn't do it."

"Oh, that's right. I keep forgetting. Your problem is you're not a psychopath. And I don't mean that in a good way. You let emotions make your decision. If more people were psychopaths, the world would be better off." Ben sat up in bed and watched as Jack paced the cell. "Wait a minute. Did you beat Bruce up before or after your little liaison in the shower? Did you guys have an amorous encounter, followed by a lover's spat?" Jack gave Bruce a smirk. "Because then it makes sense. You always hurt the ones you love. Otherwise, it makes no sense. Otherwise, you only gave Bruce a second chance to kill you. Which he is going to do."

"People saw what I can do. What I'm willing to do. They will leave me alone." Jake glanced down the hallway. Several more inmates had gathered around the railings and were whispering.

"The only ones who will leave you alone, the ones scared of you, would never bother you in the first place. But now, people see killing the person who kicked the shit out of Bruce as a way to get cred. A way to get in good with Rupert."

"You keep talking about Rupert. Who the hell is he?"

"You'll find out soon enough. Or if Bruce gets to you, maybe you will never find out."

"So, I have to worry about every two-bit con?"

"Nah. Bruce is going to want to kill you himself. Rupert will ensure nobody messes with you until Bruce has his shot."

"Who is Rupert?"

"He has 'SS' tattooed on his neck. He holds court by the weights in the prison yard." Ben picked up his book and opened it to a part where the corners had been bent. "You have two choices. Talk to Rupert, and let him know he can count on you in the future. You will still have to deal with Bruce, but Rupert will ensure it is a fair fight."

"Then Rupert owns me. No thanks." Jake slammed his hand against the wall.

"He was going to own you eventually, anyway."

"You said two choices."

"Kill Bruce on your own. Of course, it won't be a fair fight. Bruce will want to put the shiv in you himself. But he will have plenty of help. They will most likely pin you somewhere or block you from retreating. Maybe even hold you down so Bruce can kill you slowly. You should have finished him when you had the chance."

"Maybe the guards can help?"

"You have become the guards' number one pain in the ass. Right now, they are filling out paperwork and explaining how Bruce hurt himself when he slipped in the shower. And they know you are a dead man walking. They will not want to be anywhere near when you get killed." Ben turned a page of his book. "Do you know how bad it looks on their record if an inmate is killed in front of them?

Rupert will make sure they know when to make themselves scarce."

14) RUPERT

The prison yard was a large open area with three sides surrounded by a twenty-foot chin-linked fence topped with razor wire. On the fourth side was the prison's brick wall. The ground was hard-packed dirt, pounded down by hundreds of prisoners walking over it daily.

There was a basketball court which the Blacks controlled. The Whites controlled the free weights, and the Hispanics had a section where they could play handball against the prison wall. Segregation was alive and well, but it wasn't racism as you think about it in the outside world. They were equal but separate. And that's the way they wanted it. In any society, you divide into tribes, and race was the easiest way to do it.

Rupert sat on a picnic table near the weights. He was a lanky man with 'SS' tattooed on his neck. Several of his lieutenants sat around him. Occasionally, someone would approach him, and Rupert would give a slight nod or a hard stare. It was all the communication needed. He was ruling on the day-to-day issues involved in running a prison gang. Looking at him, there was nothing to indicate he should be the leader, but there it was; he had absolute control of his crew. People lived or died with nothing more than a nod.

Rupert signaled an inmate who was sitting on a bench. The inmate was a small skinny man who had several nervous ticks. As Rupert spoke to him, he looked in Jake's direction. He nodded, showing he understood, and scurried across the prison yard, headed toward Jake.

"He wants to talk to you," the inmate said as he scratched his neck.

"Who?" Jake replied.

"Who do you think, dipshit?" The inmate motioned toward Rupert.

"I don't know him. What does he want?"

"Shit. Everyone knows Rupert. Now come on. He wants to talk."

Jake watched Rupert for a few seconds. Rupert ignored him, signaled for one of his lieutenants, and dispatched him on some type of errand.

The inmate took a few steps toward Rupert, turned around, and motioned for Jake to follow. Jake sighed and strolled over to Rupert.

"I have a job for you," said Rupert. He stared into Jake's eyes, forcing Jake to look away.

"No thanks. I'm just here to do my time. And mind my own business," Jake said.

"Your time. Don't you have life with no parole?"

"I'm appealing. It should be overturned soon."

An inmate standing close by let out a laugh. Rupert gave him a sharp look, and the inmate lowered his head.

"Bruce is being released from the infirmary tomorrow. I'm not going to interfere with what is between you and Bruce. That is for you two to work out." Rupert spat some tobacco juice on the ground. He noticed Jake's surprise at Rupert's use of tobacco. "Me and the guards have an understanding. They look the other way on a lot of shit. And I make sure things don't get too out of hand. Of course, they understand sometimes scores have to be settled."

"Thanks for the offer. But I'm going to keep to myself."

"If you work for me, then it is one-on-one with you and Bruce. And I hear you can handle yourself. But if you're an outsider. Well, we look after each other."

"All the same."

Rupert frowned, shook his head, and looked away. One of his lieutenants stepped in between Jake and Rupert, forcing Jake to take a few steps back. The conversation was over. Jake strolled over to the yard's other side and sat on a bench. He looked back and saw several of Rupert's gang laughing.

Laying under the bench was a good size branch that had blown into the yard. It was about an inch across and eight inches long. Jake picked it up and hid it under his clothes.

Ben sat down next to Jake. The two of them looked straight ahead without talking. Finally, Jake said, "He wants me to join his little gang."

"Not a bad idea. You still have to kill Bruce. But at least it will be one-on-one," Ben said.

"I'm not going to kill anyone." Jake adjusted the stick he was hiding under his clothes.

"Bruce will probably kill you first, anyway. You're not going to catch him by surprise again."

"I'll protect myself. But I'm not going to start anything." Jake adjusted the stick he was hiding under his clothes.

"You're dead then." Ben spit on the ground. "Here is what will happen. Two guys will get behind you. Then Bruce will come at you. You won't be able to retreat, and when Bruce gets close, they will grab your arms. Bruce will slice you up." Ben looked at the clouds forming off in the distance. "It's a shame. I got used to you as a cellmate. It will be a pain in the ass breaking in the next guy. If you ask me, you're being inconsiderate."

"You'll survive," Jake said. "Besides, what do you expect me to do?"

"Go after him. Take the initiative. At least it will

be one-on-one. Don't let yourself be boxed in. You can't wait for him to make the first move."

"I could wrestle him to the ground. Hold him until the guards can intervene."

"The guards aren't going to do shit. There are a couple of them to hundreds of prisoners. They make a shit wage. Do you think they will risk their lives to save your sorry ass? A murderer and a rapist."

"I told you I didn't do it."

"So, you keep saying. It doesn't matter. You're here, aren't you?"

Jake looked around the prison yard. About ten percent belong here, genuinely belong here. They were predators, and the only solution was to lock them away. But the rest, how many of them started out as kids, made a stupid mistake. Maybe something as simple as selling a little pot. They get thrown into this cesspool, and what choice did they have, adapt, become a bitch, or die. Jake knew prison would be a hard life, but he didn't realize how much it corrodes a person's humanity. How it strips away your belief in people. How it leaves you only seeing the rotting spirit, the decaying hearts, and most troubling, the shuttering of the mind.

Jake wanted his life back, to be free, but he also wanted his ignorance back. To be unaware that this place existed, to only have a caricature of prison. He wanted his soul to be washed clean. But it was too late. He could walk out today, and the stench will always be with him.

Ben was telling the truth. Bruce would attack him, and he would kill him without hesitation and with malice. Or die in the process.

15) STICK

It wasn't much of a weapon, but it would have to do. Jake worked the end until he had a sharp point. The stick had good weight, and at about an inch thick, it won't break on impact. It would be best to try for soft tissue, find a vein to open up. Once again, Jake would have to rely on speed rather than brute force. He would need to try to get in several jabs before Bruce can react. It was a long shot, but it was his only option.

"What are you going to use that for? Pick his teeth?" Ben asked. "That isn't going to do you any good. Bruce is going to have a better shank. You're as good as dead."

"It's all I got," Jake said. He placed the stick in his waistband and practiced pulling it out while making a stabbing motion. They had released Bruce from the infirmary, and today would be the first time Jake saw him since the shower incident.

"If my new cellmate is an asshole, I will spit on your grave." Ben picked up a copy of a bible that Jake kept by his bed. He flipped through the pages and set it down. He then picked up a comb and examined it. "The worst part is you don't have anything I want. When a prisoner dies, his cellmate gets dibs on his possessions. Pretty selfish of you not to have anything worth taking."

"I don't plan to die. And keep your sweaty paws off my stuff." Jake hid the sharpened stick in his waistband.

"Just so I understand. You're planning to take on the biggest, ugliest, smelliest inmate in this prison with a stick? You know he is going to kill you."

"Thanks for pointing that out for the tenth time."

Ben stopped Jake at the cell door. "Listen. You're an asshole. You're arrogant, you're stubborn, you're standoffish. And I said you didn't snore. But you do. I didn't tell you because I didn't want to affect your self-esteem. It's not really a snore, more like a whimper. But don't let that worry you. Better men than you have whimpered during the night. I hear that Winston Chur—"

"Does this have a point?"

"What I'm saying is you can take this guy. He's big but slow," Ben said. "And don't worry. I'm not touching your comb. I think you have lice."

As Jake headed to the yard, George, the inmate in the next cell, asked Ben, "Do you really think he can take him?"

"No. He's dead," Ben said. "Do you want to buy a comb?"

"It doesn't matter. One less rapist in the world,"

George said. "I guess he is getting what he deserves."

"Watch your mouth. He deserves a lot better than this. Jake didn't rape anyone. The first person I've met that I actually believe is innocent. Strange, I forgot what a decent person looks like," Ben said. "In a few months, this place would have beaten that decency out of him. Maybe it's better he dies while he still has his soul."

16) THE YARD

In the yard, the other inmates were keeping their distance. Jake walked toward the nearest group and smiled as they scattered. He found a spot and stood with his back to the wall. He watched as Bruce talked with Rupert. Several times, Bruce looked in Jake's direction. Three inmates stood nearby. Rupert called them over and spoke with them for a few seconds. They all looked at Jake and nodded.

Two of them headed across the yard to Jake's left, and the other headed toward his right side. Bruce smiled and headed straight toward Jake. His face was still bruised, and what few teeth he had were gone. His smile revealed black and purple gums.

Jake had seriously injured Bruce in the shower. But stopped short and did not finish the job. This time would be different. In a few minutes, either Bruce or he would lie dead. The remaining inmates formed a large semi-circle, vying for a view of the action. A few were placing bets. Typically, there would be a lot more betting action, but everyone assumed Bruce would make quick work of Jake. No guards were in sight.

Jake felt for his sharpened stick and tucked his shirt behind it. He needed to pull it out in one swift movement. The four of them closed in on Jake. The ones positioned to his sides were preparing to pin him down, allowing Bruce to stab him.

Three-quarters of the way across, Bruce pulled out an ice pick. Jake noted Bruce's grip; it was an overhand grip, suggesting he would stab downward instead of using an underhand grip, giving him a more controlled uppercut. It was a slight advantage that Jake could exploit.

Jake waited, allowing the inmates to close in on him. When they were within three feet, Jake moved to his right, grabbed that inmate, and drove him face-first into Bruce, using him as a shield. Bruce tried to reach over and stab Jake, but Jake kept the inmate between them. Bruce made another attempt but ended up sinking the ice pick into the inmate's shoulder. Jake pulled out his sharpened stick and came over the top, pushing it into Bruce's eye.

Bruce screamed out in pain. His hand instinctively raised toward his eyes. Jake grabbed it and took the ice pick. As Bruce bent over in pain, Jake jabbed it into his neck. Blood shot out of his jugular vein. Jake pulled the ice pick out and stabbed Bruce's neck twice more. The inmates who planned to help Bruce ran into the crowd. Bruce fell to his knees, blood pooling on the ground. Jake grabbed Bruce's hair and lifted his head. He watched as the life drained from his eyes.

A jury had declared Jake a killer; now, he was one. It was easier than he thought. He did not have remorse, only contempt. He wanted to kill Bruce again and again. Every moment since his fight in the shower, he had felt regret. His hatred for Bruce had grown. He realized he had wanted this fight. He wanted to kill Bruce. Not only to remove a threat, but because of what Bruce had made him into. He was a killer, not only in deed but in his heart. Never again would he leave a job unfinished. In the future, he would always choose to kill.

Jake felt someone grab his arm, and he swung around and pointed the ice pick. It was Ben.

"Drop that thing and move. Hurry."

Ben dragged Jake twenty-five yards before a siren blared. The inmates began dropping to the ground. Ben and Jake took a couple more steps before lying flat on the ground. The inmates were instructed not to move as several guards inspected Bruce's body.

"It was self-defense," Jake said to Ben.

"No shit. But that doesn't matter," Ben said. "If you're lucky, they will throw you into solitary. If they don't, Rupert paid someone off, and they will come after you again."

"When is this going to be over? The only thing I've done is defend myself."

"Why do you keep making everything about you? It's getting a little old," Ben said. "It's never over."

Two guards approached. "You. Up. We are putting you in solitary until this is sorted out."

Jake got to his knees. "Not you. Him." They pointed at Ben.

"They want you alone in your cell," Ben whispered to Jake. "Watch out for a late-night visitor." The guards pulled Ben away. "Tell them not to get any blood on my bed."

17) ATTORNEY GENERAL

District Attorney Robert "Duke" Billings shook hands as he worked his way through the campaign staff. He frequently stopped to thank a worker and have a picture snapped of them together. People wore red, white, and blue buttons with "DUKE" in large letters.

The mood was upbeat. The latest polls showed a double-digit lead in the Attorney General race. Seen as a no-nonsense law and order candidate, the public was responding favorably. The press loved him. Giving him three times the news coverage as his opponent.

Duke never explained what he planned to do as Attorney General. But he made sure everyone knew that if they elected his opponent, crime would run rampant. There would probably be rioting in the streets. And no one would be safe. He had an amazing 85% approval rating with senior citizens.

Duke entered his office and frowned, seeing Todd Baker sitting nervously in a chair waiting for him.

Todd was the lab technician on the Jake Franklin case and had botched the DNA testing. Had Baker come forward with his error, Jake Franklin would have been acquitted, and Duke Billings' career would have been over.

"I told you I never wanted to see you again," Duke said as he walked toward a large bookshelf behind his desk. "If you need me to save your ass again, you can forget it."

"I'm sorry. It's just I see how well you're doing in the polls. You're going to be the new Attorney General." Todd fidgeted in his chair. "I don't think I should be a lab technician anymore. I mean, after what we did. It's best to put some distance between me and that job. Don't you think?"

"What I did? Do you mean how I had to fix your mistakes? How I took pity on you and didn't throw you in prison for falsifying evidence," Duke said. "If you want to quit, do it. What does that have to do with me?"

Todd clasped his hands together to keep them from shaking. "I would need a new job. A better-paying one. The Attorney General probably has lots of jobs to fill."

Duke shook his head in disbelief. "Why would I hire someone who can't do a simple lab test? Get out. And don't let the door hit you in the ass."

Todd could feel the sweat on his hands. "I would never tell anyone what we did, especially right before election day. You can count on me. One hand washes the other. It's only fair I get something in return."

"Is that some kind of weak-ass threat? Didn't you hear? There are rumors Franklin killed an inmate. I knew he was a killer. He may not have been the only one at the original murder scene. But he was involved somehow."

"I've been thinking. If I come clean. Your opponent would win. He would probably offer me a deal to testify against you. Offer probation. After all, I only did what you told me." Todd swallowed hard. "I may even get a book deal. That's how people do it. How they make lots of money."

Duke glared at Baker. He thought, *"How easy it would be to squash this guy. I could make his life a living hell. He has a lot of balls for coming here. But he is still a little weasel."*

Duke walked close and smiled as Todd flinched. He said, "You're the one who screwed up the result and then didn't tell anyone. If I go down, you go with me. And it won't be probation."

"All I did was take the new results to the DA, that was you, and the DA told me not to change the original result. The ones that showed Franklin didn't rape that woman. I was only doing what the DA, you, told me to do," Todd said as he steadied himself. "It doesn't have to be a job in your office. I'm sure you have friends who would be happy to do a favor."

Duke stared out the window. This would never go away. He had to put Todd on ice and find a way to permanently fix the problem.

"I'll see what I can do." Duke hit the intercom button. "Joan, have Hank come to my office."

Hank poked his head in the door, and Duke motioned for him to enter.

"Hank, see Mr. Baker out. Then come back. We have some matters to discuss."

"I'm leaving. Please get back to me soon," Todd said. "Do you mind if I take some of your campaign flyers and pass them out?"

Todd offered his hand to shake, but Duke only stared at him. Todd wiped his hand on his pants, nodded at Hank, and left the office.

"What did he want?" asked Hank.

"He is trying to put the squeeze on me. He wants a job. I didn't think the little shit had it in him," Duke said. "Unfortunately, we may have to give him one. That's the thanks I get for doing him a favor. For trying to be a good guy. Who do we know that won't mind having a little weasel on his payroll?"

"We have a few. Once you win, there will be a lot more."

"If I want to go a different direction. Maybe use a stick rather than a carrot. Do we know someone who can help us out?"

"We do. But that is a tricky road. And once you go down it, it becomes complicated."

"Yeah. Let's get the weasel a job. At least for now."

18) WINNING BIG

The previous District Attorney Robert "Duke" Billings, now Attorney General, scanned the cheering crowd. They were waving his campaign signs and chanting 'Duke, Duke, Duke.' Several news cameras were rolling, and reporters were gathering the crowd's reactions to the stunning victory. He had won by over thirty points, unheard of in this era of tribal politics. This was despite the top of the ticket, the Governor, unexpectedly losing his race.

Wearing a dark blue suit and red tie, Duke smiled broadly and waved to the crowd. He pointed at several people and mouthed the words "Thank you."

The polls had barely closed before the press discussed if he would run for governor. Reporting on a horse race or speculating on future events was easier than shoe-leather reporting. It also got better ratings and more airtime for the reporter.

The press realized long ago that the public didn't care about the issues. They decided where they stood, the same way they picked out toilet paper, whichever slogan stuck in their mind. But picking winners and losers, why that was pure sports. And the best part, it required very little work. You could spend six months doing an in-depth analysis of the condition of prisons, and it may get printed in a magazine that nobody reads anymore. But stand before a camera, predict the next governor, and you will be on the evening news.

In the crowd, fidgeting was Todd Baker. Billings had recently arranged a plum job with a large manufacturer for Todd. The company's president had gone to college with Duke and provided the job as a favor. Todd was unaware he was about to be transferred to a factory in Mexico. He would complain, but the money was too good to refuse. Billings wanted Todd out of the way and far out of sight.

A victory celebration with key staff, friends, and large donors was underway in Duke's hotel suite. As the champagne flowed, more than a few people were getting drunk. After a long campaign, it was to be expected. There would probably be a couple of post-campaign babies or at least pregnancies. Duke frowned as he surveyed the room; he preferred bourbon and always in moderation. But they had worked hard, and it was only right to let them celebrate.

Duke motioned for Billy Cruse to come over. Billy was the college buddy who had given Todd Baker a job. In college, Duke had introduced Billy to Jennifer, who would become his wife. Duke was also responsible for getting Billy through most of his calculus classes. And more than once, drove him home after a night out. Duke had a lot of acquaintances but very few genuine friends. Billy came as close as anyone.

"Thank you for giving Baker a job," Duke said. He poured himself and Billy a bourbon. "You like it neat, If I remember correctly."

"Anything for a friend of yours," Billy said. He took the glass of bourbon from Duke.

"He's not a friend. Just someone I need out of the way," Duke said. "Does your company do drug testing?"

"We have the right to do a random test," Billy said. "But we don't unless there is a problem. We lost too many good workers because they smoked a little weed." Billy took a sip of bourbon.

"I need leverage," said Duke. "Maybe his co-workers take him out for a night on the town. The next day, he is called in for a random test."

"Does he do drugs?" Billy pulls two cigars out of his coat pocket. Offers Duke one, but Duke waves it off. Billy shrugs and puts them back.

"I'm sure you have someone who can make sure a little coke shows up. Better if he snorts the coke himself. Peer pressure is a wonderful thing," Duke said. "I wouldn't be unhappy if there was a trace amount of fentanyl."

"Sure. Then do you want me to fire Baker?"

"No. A warning will do. Make sure to document it. Build a record of an incompetent, undisciplined employee." said Duke. "Oh, make him attend some type of drug rehab. I just need leverage."

Duke smiled at his old college buddy, and Billy gave a nod.

"I hate to bring this up on your big night, but this environmental case is pending against my company. The board is getting a little nervous. Good chance to make some friends."

"When will government bureaucrats stop harassing hard-working business owners?" Duke sipped his bourbon and smiled at Billy.

"Hey, I saw Karen the other day," Billy said. "She still looks great."

"Karen. Karen?"

"Yeah. Whatever happened between you guys?"

"It was a freshman thing. You know, new on campus, didn't know anybody. It would never have worked. She is too independent. The fights we had. Just couldn't get her to listen."

Hank, Duke's campaign manager, approached. He shook hands with Billy and asked for a few minutes with the new Attorney General. Duke slapped Billy on the back and shook his hand. Billy congratulated Duke and headed across the room.

"They are already talking about a run for governor," Hank said. "The press is leading all their broadcasts with the possibility."

"It's easier than doing real reporting," Duke said. "Which one can we give an exclusive interview to? Someone who will softball my new tough-on-crime initiative."

"Take your pick," Hank said. "We have two or three with enough smarts to know if they play ball; they can be reporting from the Governor's mansion in four years."

Duke watched as a staff member stumbled and spilled his drink.

"Make sure everyone drinking takes an Uber home," Duke said. "Last thing we need is one of my staff getting a DUI, or worse." Duke took a sip of his bourbon. "Governor, you say. I like the way it sounds."

19) HOBART

The warden's office had that old administration building feel. It had large, thick glass-plated windows and heavy plaster walls. An old fan slowly rotated on the ceiling, too high to reach, its blades covered in dust. The furniture was from the 1930s, and there were two large steel filing cabinets used mainly to store miscellaneous items. A half-filled bottle of whiskey and several glasses were in the top drawer. The glasses were unwashed and contained several sets of smudged fingerprints.

Pictures on the walls showed the warden shaking hands with various dignitaries. One was of him and Duke Billings, smiling for the cameras as they gave each other a firm handshake. It was snapped at a fundraiser for Billings. Hobart had charged the campaign donation to the prison, listing it as a toilet paper purchase. When the auditors questioned the transaction, Hobart explained the prisoners had taken to using large amounts of toilet paper as a means of protest. The auditors were unsatisfied with the answer but had no means of verification.

Warden Hobart put the phone down and sat at his desk, staring into space. He had just finished updating Billings on Bruce's death. At first, Billings was adamant that Franklin be charged. Hobart had patiently explained to Billings that would mean putting Franklin in solitary. There would be another trial. Franklin would claim self-defense and most likely be found innocent. The press would bring up his first conviction, and Franklin would repeat his claims that the DNA evidence was corrupt. You say something enough times, and people begin to believe it. A small but active group was already spreading a conspiracy theory.

Billings said, "Do what you think best. But a lid needs to be put on Franklin." He then hung up by slamming the phone down.

Across from Hobart sat the prison medical director and two prison guards. They were waiting to hear how the warden wanted to handle the incident. Inmates died in prison. That was a fact of life. But when one inmate killed another, that raised all kinds of questions. Usually, an outside investigator was involved. Hobart wanted to avoid that; an independent investigation can have unexpected results. Better to keep it in-house.

"Doctor, if someone falls, say they slip in the shower, isn't there a chance that blood clots form?" Hobart asked. He gave a hopeful look at the medical director and nodded his head, encouraging him to agree.

"Yes. In certain cases, it can be deadly, causing a heart attack or a stroke," the doctor said. "Someone overweight and in poor health. As Bruce was, it is highly likely."

"So, it's not out of the question that Bruce's recent fall in the shower caused a blood clot to travel to his brain, and he died of a stroke."

One guard laughed. "That or a stick in the eye." He gave a light punch in the shoulder to the other guard.

The warden ignored the guards and looked at the medical director.

"I won't know until I do the autopsy. But I think the results will confirm your suspicion."

"Good. And do the cremation right away. I think it will comfort the family, knowing we have properly put him to rest."

"And don't forget to pull the stick out of his eye," a guard said. He laughed and looked around. Everyone stared at him. "I mean, it was tragic what happened. He was so young." The warden glared at the guard, his lips tightly pressed together. "He will be missed," the guard said, lowering his head.

The other guard leaned forward and said, "Rupert wants to handle Franklin. He's upset about losing Bruce. Bruce did a lot of heavy lifting for Rupert. It will be hard to replace him."

"What is he planning?" Hobart asked. "I promised

Billings I would handle Franklin. That guy is becoming a pain in my ass."

"Hasn't decided. Rupert wants to talk with Franklin first," the guard said. "He also mentioned one of his outside contacts would compensate you for the trouble."

"Okay. Let the prisoners sort out their own problems," Hobart said. "I have to contact Bruce's next of kin. If he has one."

20) SECOND CHANCE

Jake had expected to be charged with Bruce's death. But none of the guards saw the incident. They had made themselves scarce on a tip from Rupert. As far as they were concerned, this was a matter to be settled between inmates. Of course, they expected Jake would be the one lying dead.

During the day, cell doors remained open, and inmates were free to interact. Jake was lying on his bunk when he received a visitor. Rupert walked around the cell, examining Jake's meager possessions. Inmates don't have much, but most have a few items. Maybe some decent slippers, a radio, or a box of crackers. But other than a bible, Jake had next to nothing. Only what the prison issued, nothing from the commissary. Everything of value belonged to his cellmate Ben.

Rupert picked up the bible and flipped through the pages. "Somewhere in here, it says an eye for an eye."

Jake did not make eye contact with Rupert and said, "Leviticus 24, as he has done, it shall be done to him, fracture for fracture, eye for eye, tooth for tooth; whatever injury he has given a person shall be given to him."

"I had you pegged as Matthew 5:38, 'You have heard that it was said, An eye for an eye and a tooth for a tooth. But I say to you, Do not resist the one who is evil,'" Rupert put the bible down. "Not saying I'm evil. But sometimes, I go to confession."

"Did you come here for bible study?" Jake sarcastically asked as he sat up.

"No. I'm here because you took something away from me. Bruce did a lot of work for me. The way I see it that all falls on you now."

"I'm just here to do my time. Mind my own business."

"So, you keep saying. But it seems you spend a lot of that time beating the crap out of people," said Rupert. "You will be compensated for your service. We have people on the outside that will keep your commissary account flush. And you won't have to worry about anyone messing with you. That includes the guards."

"Like I said—"

"I know. But give it some thought. You have shown you can handle yourself. But surprise is no longer on your side. Next time, it won't be so easy." Rupert walked to the cell door, turned, and said, "I'm going to have them put $100 in your account. Get yourself a decent robe and some slippers."

"Keep it. Not interested."

"You may want to read Ezekiel 25:17."

"Don't need to. I saw Pulp Fiction."

"Make sure you get a good night's sleep," Rupert said, walking away.

The inmate in the next cell entered and said, "Are you crazy? That was a personal visit by Rupert. You can't say no. No one ever says no."

"I just did," Jake said. He laid back down on his bunk and closed his eyes. Trying to remember what it was like before prison, but his mind was blank. He had traveled too far into the darkness. The connection to his old life was growing dim. He was having trouble recognizing who he once was. All his aspirations were gone. Now everything was about survival. All his mental energy was going into how to make it one more day.

"You're a dead man. I'm guessing they come for you in your sleep. They already moved Ben to solitary."

"I'll make sure the door is locked." Jake rolled on his side and scanned the cell for anything to defend himself.

"That won't stop a guard. Rupert pays a half dozen of them twice their salary. They only make a little more than McDonald's workers. He can get to you anytime he wants. Why do you think they want you alone in your cell? I bet he puts a bounty on you. They will be lining up to get a crack at you."

21) LATE ONE NIGHT

Jake lay on the top bunk, wide awake. The cellblock was mainly quiet, but there was always the occasional shout. Maybe someone having a nightmare or someone who can't sleep decided nobody else should. Sometimes the shouts were screams. But it was all background noise, barely noticed, just part of a nighttime soundscape of a prison. The same as if you were camping in the woods, and creatures were calling out to each other.

Ben, Jake's cellmate, had been taken to solitary confinement. No reason was given, but none was needed. Everyone knew Rupert had paid off the guards. He wanted Jake alone in his cell.

Jake had refused to join Rupert's jailhouse gang, which was about to result in retribution. At a minimum, he would be beaten and possibly raped. It is doubtful he would be murdered. Rupert needed to break Jake, not make him some type of martyr.

Jake wondered if dismissing Rupert's offer to join his gang was a mistake. This was the third time he would have to fight for his life. And most certainly not his last. It would never end. Jake's plan to keep his head down and do his time had failed miserably. Maybe he couldn't do this alone. Maybe he should join Rupert. But Rupert wanted an enforcer, someone to replace Bruce. It's one thing to harm a person trying to harm you. It is another to harm someone because you're paid to do it. Jake would be asked to punish future versions of himself. It wouldn't be Jake, but it would be who Jake used to be. Who he was when he entered this institution of moral decay.

How is this all possible? What had he done wrong? He had given a co-worker with too much to drink a ride home. Should he have checked her house? No, there was no reason to believe she was in danger. He only had to make sure she didn't get behind the wheel. It was a good deed. This is how he is repaid. Where is the justice? Forget the justice system; doesn't god play a part? Isn't he watching out, not asking for a favor, but shouldn't he keep the scales balanced? Give a person half a chance.

Jake's mind drifted to the trial. The DNA evidence and that squirrely guy, the lab tech. When he testified, he seemed confident. But then he was in the courtroom while the jury deliberated. He was nervous, and his shirt was drenched in sweat. He kept looking at Billings. And Billings, the scowl on his face when he saw him. The lab tech's eyes were pleading with Billings. Those two knew something. They had figured out that the DNA evidence was tainted. That had to be it. They knew it wasn't Jake's DNA. And Billings still sent him to prison. Who is the real criminal?

And there was that guy in the back of the courtroom. The one who smiled at Jake as if they had something in common. Jake had seen him before. He was sure it was at the bar the night Suzy James was killed. Was he the murderer? With all the news cameras, there would be pictures of him. *"If only I could hire a private investigator,"* Jake thought. *"How come no one else can see all the unanswered questions, all the loose ends?"*

Jake knew the answer. He was part of a system that cannot admit it made a mistake. There was no quality control, no one to do an independent audit. What would happen if they randomly selected a hundred cases and did a full review? How many would be innocent, and what would be an acceptable error rate, 2%, 5%? Jake's life, his freedom, his dignity, all destroyed, representing nothing more than an acceptable margin of error.

If Jake was going to be attacked, the cell door would have to be opened. One or more guards must be on Rupert's payroll. Rupert was a high-ranking member of a criminal organization. They could easily reach inside the prison walls. Shit, they could reach anyone, inside or outside the prison. And they had enough cash to buy off any guard who was so inclined. And a surprisingly large number of guards were so inclined. Or maybe it wasn't so surprising, considering the low wages and inadequate training the State provided.

When Jake couldn't sleep, he would stare at Ben's clock radio and watch the minutes slowly tick away. That wasn't possible tonight; the radio was gone from the shelf. Jake had other uses for it.

Before the nightly lockdown, the guards swept the prison cells, looking for weapons and contraband. This wasn't uncommon, but tonight's timing suggested they wanted to ensure Jake did not have a shank or other weapon. They spent more time than usual in his cell.

They found nothing, but after lights out, Jake broke apart the clock radio. He ended up with a four-inch sharp plastic shard. It would be no good for stabbing, but it could slice across a vein. The electric cord would also be helpful. He would owe Ben a new clock radio. Ben would complain about it but, under the circumstances, would understand.

The sound of keys jingled outside his cell door. Two men were whispering to each other. One was a guard, the other his muscle. They were giddy with excitement. The guard took several tries to put the key in the door.

"You hold him down. Rupert wants a message sent," the inmate said to the guard. "It is going to be a long, painful night for our little friend."

The guard laughed and pulled out his nightstick.

Both men entered the cell, and the guard closed the door, keys still hanging from the lock.

"Why is the floor so wet?" the inmate asked.

"Maybe he pissed himself," the guard said as they advanced toward the bunk.

Jake rolled over in his bunk and dumped a bucket of water on an already-soaked floor. His other hand held the cord from the clock radio. The wires were stripped clean on one end, and the other was plugged into the wall socket. He dropped the cord onto the flooded floor. A blue electric flash swept across the floor, and the two men collapsed. The smell of hair being singed filled the cell. Jake waited a few seconds before pulling a string that yanked the cord from the wall. He jumped from the bunk and rolled the guard over. The guard was stunned and struggled to regain his bearings. Jake took the plastic shard and cut across the guard's neck. Blood, first a trickle, then a stream, and finally a spurt shot out.

Jake rolled over the inmate. Severe electrical burns covered his face. He was no longer breathing. The electrical shock had killed him instantly.

Jake's body count was now three. All self-defense, all fending off attackers who aimed to do him serious harm. Jake was under no illusion that justice would prevail.

Jake took the guard's handcuffs, went outside his cell, and closed and locked the door. He then waved at the cameras to get the other guards' attention. Jake put the handcuffs on himself, showed his hands to the cameras, dropped to the floor, and laid face down, his cuffed hands covering his head. After a few minutes, he saw three guards running toward him.

The guards saw the two men dead inside Jake's cell. One of them, a fellow guard. They kicked and hit Jake with their nightsticks. The beating went on for several minutes until more guards arrived.

Barely alive, they dragged Jake to the infirmary.

22) INFIRMARY

It had been over a month since the incident. Jake had internal bleeding, cracked ribs, and was in a coma. They had initially sent him to a hospital, where they operated to stop the internal bleeding. Twice he almost died and had to be revived. The prison guards sent to watch over him tried to convince the doctors to let him die, but each time Jake pulled through. One guard still had traces of blood on his shoe from the beating he had administered to Franklin.

Once he stabilized, they sent him back to the prison infirmary to recover. The trip back was in an old prison van, and the guards took every opportunity to hit potholes. Several times the prison doctor complained, but the guards only smiled and laughed.

The infirmary was a rectangular room with five beds on each side. Along the back wall were two examination rooms. They had converted one of the two to hold Jake Franklin. A State Police officer sat inside the room reading an old Golf Digest magazine. The officer was not there to prevent Franklin from escaping. There was no need for that. Jake had not moved since they placed him in the bed, and it was questionable if he would recover. The officer was there to ensure the prison guards did not finish what they started and kill Franklin.

The prison guards knew Franklin was only defending himself, but that did not matter. He had killed one of their own, and several were determined to kill Franklin in return. The warden would have turned a blind eye to the guards' vigilante pursuits and let them complete the cycle of violence. But Attorney General Duke Billings had taken an interest in the incident and dispatched State Police to guard Franklin. Billings made it clear he did not want Franklin to die at the hands of a prison guard. He had other plans.

23) PRISON TOUR

Attorney General Duke Billings arrived at the prison shortly before nine in the morning. The local station sent a small camera crew to cover the visit. Billings made a brief speech outlining his get tough on Crime initiative. He called for more prison cells and the need to stop coddling prisoners. He thanked the press and informed them they could not accompany him inside. Explaining it was for their safety.

His real purpose was to check on Jake and see how bad the situation was. Duke wanted Jake to recover so that he could stand trial for the murder of the guard. He wanted to show everyone that his initial conviction took a dangerous man off the street. To remove any doubt that Jake Franklin was a murderer. If Jake died, it would go unnoticed. But a trial where this dangerous prisoner is convicted of a second murder would play well in the press. And Billings would be there to claim the credit. After all, he was the one who got Jake Franklin off the streets.

A second conviction would also keep Jake imprisoned even if his original conviction was thrown out because of faulty DNA evidence. The last thing Duke needed was for Jake to appear on the news channels, saying Billings had wrongly convicted him. Duke wanted to show the public that Jake was nothing but a cold-hearted killer. This would help Duke's planned run for the Governorship. As the one who put Jake away in the first place, it would add credence to his law-and-order stance.

It was a gamble. Letting Franklin die in prison would effectively put an end to the first trial. But the news coverage was too tempting to pass up. Besides, enough time had passed, and even if the faulty DNA evidence was uncovered, Billings could spin it so that the lab technician was at fault.

Duke stood over Jake's bed, shaking his head. Jake had a feeding tube, IVs, and a machine helping him breathe. "Shit. Your guys sure did a number on him."

"He had already killed an inmate and a guard. They did what they needed to subdue him," the warden said.

"A lot of the inmates are telling a different story. They say he was lying flat on the floor, had given himself up."

"You can't trust prisoners. They will say anything. Hoping to make a deal to reduce their time."

"Where are the tapes from the security cameras?" Duke asked.

"All the cameras were off. We had a power failure. Caused by Franklin short-circuiting the socket in his cell."

"That would explain why there was no footage after he electrocuted the two men. Why is there no footage leading up to the incident?"

The warden stood with a puzzled look on his face. He mumbled a few words, thought better, and stuttered a few more. Finally, he just stared.

"Christ," said Billings. "Maybe it is because there was no evidence on them, and you reused the tapes. Budgets are tight."

"Yeah, that's it," said the warden.

Billings shook his head. This was going to be more challenging than he thought. He knew the real story behind what happened, or at least enough to know that if the truth came out, Franklin would be cleared, and the warden and a few guards would end up on the other side of the bars. "Why was the guard in Franklin's cell?"

"He heard a disturbance and went to investigate."

"Why did he go into the cell? Is that standard practice?"

"No, but he saw the other inmate was in trouble. He was trying to help."

"What was the other inmate doing in the cell? That was not his assigned cell."

The warden stood like a deer caught in headlights.

"Holy shit. A first-year law student would tear you to shreds. And not a first-year from a respectable law school. One from an offshore correspondence school. Scratch that; a sixth grader would rip you a new one." Billings scratched his head. The warden had spent too much time isolated in this prison. He was used to total control, with nobody questioning his orders. He had grown soft, thinking his weak-ass lies were good enough for the outside world.

"We haven't completed our investigation. I may not have all the details yet." The warden looked down at his shoes.

"Listen. I want Jake Franklin convicted of killing that guard. I want him to get the death sentence. And I want it to be a clean, open and shut case."

"We all want that." The warden tried to edge toward the door. He was hoping to end Billings' questioning as soon as possible.

"This little Keystone Cop routine you have isn't going to get it done. If this case gets screwed up, you won't be a warden. You will be back doing prisoner counts."

"I'll do my best," the warden said as he held the door open.

"Your best. Is that supposed to reassure me?" Duke stared at the warden for a few minutes. "My office is taking over the investigation. I'm assigning one of my assistants to you. Your job is to do whatever he tells you. If he tells you to get on your knees and kiss his ass, that is what you do. We are not losing this case."

The warden glanced at the guards. They were looking away, trying to pretend they didn't notice the warden being dressed down by the Attorney General. He bit his lip and shook his head.

Billings glared at the warden and stormed out the door.

24) VISITOR

A doctor shined a small pin light into Jake's eyes. Jake followed the light, moving only his eyes. The doctor then ran a small metal pick across Jake's foot. Jake flinched. The doctor smiled, made several notes, and hung the chart from his bed. He glanced at a State Police officer slumping in a chair and snoring lightly. He tapped the leg of the chair, and the officer woke up, startled.

"Try to stay alert. The prisoner is not ready to leave, but if he wanted, he could have taken your gun," the doctor said.

"I was just resting my eyes. He would never have gotten close to me."

"Whatever you say." The doctor looked at Jake. "You're a lucky man. There is no permanent damage."

"Yeah, I feel lucky," Jake said.

"They want me to sign off. Say you're well enough to stand trial. But I think you're about two weeks away." The doctor turned toward the guard and said, "Step outside. I need to go over a few things with you. Don't worry; he is not going anywhere."

The doctor opened the door and waited for the guard to exit. He then held it open so an inmate with a mop and bucket could enter. Jake rolled over, turning his back to the inmate as he mopped the floor.

"Hey, asshole," Ben said. "You owe me a radio."

"Holly shit. They let you out of solitary," Jake said as he turned around and sat up.

"They needed someone to clean up the mess you left in our cell," Ben said. "Did you have to destroy my radio?"

"When I was taking it apart. I said the first thing Ben will do is bitch about his radio."

"It played both AM and FM. If it was just AM, I could let it go," Ben said. "Christ, they did a number on you."

"How is this playing out?" Jake asked.

"The guards want to kill you. But the rumor is that Billings wants you alive. He wants you to get the death penalty for killing the guard."

"They want to keep me alive so they can kill me?"

"Yep. Makes for better press," Ben said. "Billings is crawling up the warden's ass. He wants to see you convicted, something awful."

"It was self-defense. It's on all the cameras."

"You are the toughest son of a bitch, I know. But not the smartest. The tapes are gone. The fix is in.

What did you expect?"

"It's strange. After everything, I keep thinking justice will prevail. That somewhere, somebody will do the right thing. Just one person to stand up and tell the truth."

"Maybe they would if it did any good. But one person would get chewed up, just like you. You're up against the system, and the system knows how to protect itself."

"Is Rupert after me?"

"He got paroled. Thanks to you. They didn't want anyone around who may tell a different story. Not that Rupert would. He is smart enough to keep his mouth shut. But the warden isn't taking chances."

"So, no more worrying about the prisoners?"

"Hell, you're their hero now. Won't do you any good. Nobody is stupid enough to tell the truth. But maybe they will name their kids after you," Ben said. "I have to go. Hey, are you going to eat your pudding cup? We don't get those in General Population."

"Take it. But we are even on the radio."

"What? It's butterscotch. Maybe if it was chocolate," Ben said. "Hang in there. You've come this far. Don't let the bastards get you."

25) TRIAL

Jake Franklin sat next to his court-appointed lawyer. The lawyer was busy typing messages into his phone. Jake tried to ask him about the possibility of filing an appeal, but he ignored him. As far as his lawyer was concerned, this was an unpleasant task that he needed to perform, and the sooner it was over, the better.

The lawyer had tried to convince Jake to plead guilty. If he did so, he might get life in prison instead of the death penalty. After all, what difference did it make? He was already serving life in prison. Jake refused, insisting it was self-defense. Throughout the trial, the lawyer complained to Jake that he was wasting his and the court's time.

As the jury filed in, most of them averted their eyes. A couple of them glared at Jake as if to say you're going to get what's coming to you. Jake didn't need to hear the verdict. He knew what it would be. He knew what it would be before the trial started.

It was supposed to be a jury of his peers. The jury contained a few old ladies, an old man, and a collection of suburban cul-de-sac dwellers. How were these his peers? How could they relate? How could they know what it was like inside? Did any of them ever have to fight for their lives? Their biggest concern was the neighbor's dog taking a dump on their lawn. Did any of them lie in bed, caged up, waiting for a guard and inmate to attack? Of course, he killed them, and of course, he took extreme measures. What choice did he have? It was kill or be killed. Give him a jury of inmates, his true peers; they would understand he did the minimum necessary to survive. In this case, the minimum necessary was to kill both men in whatever manner he could. It wasn't a gruesome murder. It was self-defense.

But the prosecution presented a steady stream of manufactured evidence. A new cellmate was put in Jake's cell. They hadn't had time to do the paperwork since it happened earlier on the day in question. Jake attacked the cellmate. The guard opened the door to break up the fight. Jake shoved an exposed electrical cord into the guard's chest. The guard was knocked out, and Jake used a jagged piece of plastic to saw through the guard's jugular. He then electrocuted his new cellmate.

It was all lies. The guards knew it, the prosecutor knew it, and the jury should have known it. Jake was tired of people deciding what they wanted to be true rather than learning what was true. You swear an oath. When did truth become meaningless? When did it become okay to choose your own facts, to believe what you wanted to believe, rather than what happened? Isn't it a sin to bear false witness? If you didn't want to obey your oath, can't you at least follow the ninth commandment?

One guard and several inmates testified to the facts as presented by the prosecution. Their testimony, along with the case, was full of holes. Shortly after the trial, the guard would be promoted, and the inmates would be paroled. The fix was in, but no one cared. Not the judge, not the men giving false witness, not the jury, not even his court-appointed defense attorney. It was all a play, everyone performing their part, striving to a predetermined end.

Jake testified on his own behalf. It was against the advice of his council, but he wanted the facts on the record. The prosecutor sat smirking, and the judge rolled his eyes. The guard's widow yelled, "Murderer." Lightly tapping his gavel, the judge said, "Order."

It took the jury less than twenty minutes to return a guilty verdict. Before the judge passed the sentence, he allowed the victims to speak. The guard's wife talked about how her husband was a simple, hardworking man. How he never harmed anyone and had great compassion for the prisoners. That he had dedicated his life in hopes that they could be rehabilitated. And this was how he was repaid.

She didn't mention that they lived in a 3500-foot house in an affluent neighborhood, that she drove a BMW, and he drove a GMC Hummer capable of towing their large boat. They took vacations twice a year, once to the Caribbean, the other to Las Vegas. All on a guard's salary. Jake had tried to get his defense attorney to bring this up during the trial. But the judge ruled it immaterial.

The judge completed the charade by handing down the death penalty. He frowned and said, "Jake Franklin, having been found guilty by a jury of your peers, you are hereby sentenced to death at a time and in a manner prescribed by law. May the lord show you more mercy than you have shown your victims."

Duke Billings, who was sitting in the back, smiled. He was there to show his support for law enforcement. But more importantly, every news channel in the state was covering the trial. Billings had prepared a statement and would claim that justice had been done. His only complaint was that it took too long to carry out an execution.

Jake's attorney closed his briefcase and shook the prosecutor's hand. Jake watched as the two smiled and laughed about some unrelated event.

Two guards lifted Jake from his chair and hauled him out of the courtroom. A cameraman stuck a microphone in front of Jake and asked for a comment.

"I'm innocent. I was innocent in the first case, and this one was self-defense," Jake said.

The guards pushed the cameraman away and shoved Jake into a waiting prison van. This time, they would put him into solitary confinement until it was time to be executed.

26) DEATH ROW

The cell was six by nine feet with no window, only a bunk and a metal toilet. Although Jake was supposed to get one hour a day outside, most days he did not. They left the lights on twenty-four hours a day, and it became impossible to determine when one day ended and another began. He tried to keep count of his meals, but some days they would simply not feed him. The worse part was the boredom. He had nothing to read and no one to talk to. His sanity was at stake, and Jake held on by a thread. His lawyer later told him he spent forty-five days in solitary before they moved him to death row. That was three years ago.

Death Row had over a hundred prisoners waiting to be executed. Ohio had problems getting the drugs needed to humanly put the prisoners to death. After the last execution, there was a debate on whether the prisoner had felt pain. A witness swore they had seen him flinch. The Governor placed a moratorium on executions until a full review could be completed. Duke Billings, who has entered the Governor's race, has pledged to resume executions as soon as he takes office. He pledged Ohio would become the number one state in executions. The public took little interest either way.

Jake had no compassion for his fellow death row inmates. Most of them had long ago given up claiming their innocence. Many like to relive their murders and go over every detail to anyone who would listen. When the guards were not around, some would talk about how they wanted to be free so they could kill again. As far as Jake was concerned, line up the whole bunch and have a firing squad free up some cell space.

He realized the irony of this. He was innocent and trying as hard as possible to stay alive. But he wasn't doing it, so he could spend the rest of his life in a cell. Jake wanted to clear his name and people to know the truth and expose the corruption. He wasn't afraid of dying; he was afraid of wasting away in prison. Afraid the people who wrongly put him here would never have to answer for their crimes.

Michael Crane was a tall, slim, well-dressed young lawyer from the Freedom Foundation. They were an organization that opposed the death penalty and handled inmates' appeals pro-bono. They assigned him to handle Jake's appeals. He had slowly pieced the truth together. It wasn't difficult. Prisoners and guards were willing to talk off the record about what happened. In fact, the prisoners regularly talked about it among themselves. Jake Franklin had become a hero to them. Someone who wasn't willing to take any shit. But nobody was willing to talk on the record. And those who did speak up were very accident-prone. Michael Crane had become convinced that Jake Franklin acted in self-defense. But knowing this did no good. The best he could do was file appeals and delay the death sentence.

Crane was dealing with a situation he had not encountered before. Judges denied his appeals in record time. Often without a hearing. He suspected influential people were intervening and wanted to see Jake executed as soon as possible. On average, inmates spent twenty years before their appeals had been exhausted. At the rate Crane was going, Franklin would be executed within a year.

"I need you to look into the first case," Jake said. "If you want to help me, find out why I was a match for the DNA."

"Not this again," Crane said. "Even if the first conviction is overturned, you will still be executed for killing the guard. I'm supposed to spend my time on the death penalty case. My organization doesn't handle other cases."

"It's all connected. Duke Billings was the District Attorney on the first case. And You can bet he is the one behind pushing to have me executed as soon as possible," Jake said. "Billings knows that DNA was tainted. He let me be convicted, despite knowing. Now he is trying to get rid of all the loose ends. And I'm the biggest of the loose ends."

Crane had graduated from law school with a healthy skepticism about the legal system. He knew innocent people got convicted for crimes they did not commit. But he believed it was due to mistakes, poor representation, and the failure of some juries not to think critically. What Jake was talking about was a full-blown conspiracy. One that involved the Attorney General. He knew something wasn't right. But couldn't believe it had reached that height.

"I have raised your concerns with senior members of my firm. They have instructed me to only focus on the death row case. In fact, they want to pull me for more promising cases."

Jake stared at Michael for a long minute. "So, why are you here?"

"I'm trying to save your life."

"No. You're trying to stop them from executing me. But then what? I spend the rest of my life in a cage. Eating what they tell me to eat. Shitting where they tell me to shit. Getting a court-ordered one hour of exercise a day. Life in prison is not an improvement over execution. I believe in the death penalty. If I was guilty, I would roll up my sleeve and smile while they injected me. What I don't believe in is letting incompetent, corrupt public servants imprison innocent people."

"Look, I think it was self-defense. I think the guard

was corrupt. Shit, he was living a lifestyle like he was a millionaire. Something is not right here. But there is only so much I can do."

"And it starts with the first case and Duke Billings," Jake said. "You do what you want. But don't fool yourself. If you are here to file paperwork with the court. Then that's what you do. And these conversations are useless. If you are fighting for justice, searching for truth, you will have to get your hands dirty and start doing a hell of a better job."

Jake stood up and motioned for the guard to take him back. As he walked toward the door, Michael called out, "Did you rape and murder that woman? Did you do it?"

Jake stood, his back to Michael. He had answered this question so many times. "No."

"Why did your DNA match?"

"Find that out, and you will have overturned your first wrongful conviction." Jake left the room.

Michael sat at the table, staring off into space. It was much more than a feeling that Jake was telling the truth. Michael had a deep-down belief that Jake was innocent. Innocent of everything. Innocent of the rape, innocent of the murder of the woman, and innocent of the murder of the guard. He felt helpless.

27) CANDIDATE BILLINGS

Clay Mason lived in a stone Tudor house on a hundred-acre estate, hidden in a grove of trees well off the road. The driveway snaked through manicured lawns, tennis courts, a swimming pool, and a large horse barn. Mason was one of the most powerful men in the country, but very few people knew about him. He operated behind the scenes and was the bridge between the different worlds. Mason had connections in the political, business, religious, academic, scientific, entertainment, sports, and every other group with money or power. He is agnostic on most issues. The only thing he believes in is power. He is a broker but doesn't deal with stocks and bonds. He deals in favors and people's lives. Due to Mason, dozens of men and women live a rich and successful life, and a similar number lie in ruin because they crossed him.

He is invisible to the public, but his deeds aren't. They are in plain view, a public figure, or a celebrity, is on top of the world, seemingly they have everything, and then come crashing down.

The cause is never what the press says. The real reason is they failed to keep a promise or accommodate a favor.

Duke Billings was greeted by Mason's assistant and guided to a library, where Mason sat reading a leather-bound book. The personal assistant cleared her throat, and Mason looked up from his book, smiled, and motioned for Billings to have a seat.

"Have you ever read Fountainhead?" asked Mason. "Some people say Atlas Shrugged is her best work. But I disagree."

"No. I don't get much time to read," Billings said. Duke was offended that Mason did not raise to greet him and offer to shake hands. And even though Duke only drank in moderation, it was customary to ask if your guest wanted a drink. If it was too early for alcohol, then coffee.

"What brings you all the way out here?" Mason asked. "I would show you around. But in a bit of a time crunch today. I'm meeting Jimmy Jenkins later today."

There it was. Duke had come to ask Mason for his support in the Governor's race. And Mason had just told Duke he was supporting Jenkins instead. The not standing, no handshake, no drink, and now dropping his name. Not only was he going to support Jenkins, he was about to tell Duke he shouldn't run.

"Jenkins has done a lot of good work lately," Mason said. "Don't you think he would make a fine governor? The donors love him."

"Sure. Someday. But he still needs some seasoning," Billings said.

"Seasoning? He is older than you," Mason said, picking up his book. "So, what can I do for you?"

"I wanted you to be the first to know. I'm running for Governor. I'm hoping I have your support."

"Have you seen the polls? I know you still have a small lead. But your numbers are going in the wrong direction. Our large donors are nervous about you. Duke, you have too heavy of a hand when dealing with problems. You need to learn a little finesse. You're doing a fine job as Attorney General. The State would benefit from you serving another term."

"The people appreciate a strong leader," Billings said. "I hope I have your support. But I'm running either way."

Mason opened his book and began reading. "Take a few apples on your way out. We have a wonderful orchard behind the barn."

As Billings left Mason's estate, he thought about what running would mean without his support. The big donors would ignore him, and half of the press would suddenly run negative stories. It was another example of people trying to screw him.

It would make it a much more challenging race, but Mason would come around if his poll numbers improved. Duke knew how to repay favors, and in the end, that is what counts.

28) GOVERNOR

The celebration on election night was muted. The atmosphere was more of a relief than a victory party. Everyone had been expecting for weeks that Duke Billings would win by a large margin. But as the results came in, it was clear that his supporters stayed home, and his opponents flooded the polls. Halfway through the evening, when it looked like he might actually lose, he had his staff plant stories of election irregularities. In the end, Duke Billings won, but barely. There would be recounts, but his victory should hold.

In the election's closing days, there was a steady stream of news stories concerning his heavy-handed tactics. It caused many independent voters to stay home. Ultimately, he won, but the news narrative was that he was damaged goods. Despite a small core of loyal votes, many voters had grown weary of his never-ending drama.

Billings suspected Clay Mason had something to do with the news stories. But since he won, he would have plenty to offer Mason. It would not take long to get back in his good graces. The news stories were Mason's way of letting Billings know he still had considerable power.

The television blurted out, "Duke Billings, once a rising star in his party, now may be seen as more of a liability. His minuscule margin of victory over the unpopular incumbent has shown the once unstoppable Billings has lost favor with the voters."

"Turn that crap off," Billings said. "I won, and they are making it sound like my career is over." Duke opened the blinds on the window and looked out over the Governor's Mansion lawn. He had worked all his life to reach this point, but it wasn't enough. There was one more step. He had hoped his victory would be so overwhelming that two years from now, he would get his party's nomination for President becoming the youngest man to win the office. Now he would not even get the VP nomination. It was the fickle voter's fault. One minute they want a strong leader; the next, they complain about strong-arm tactics.

Duke sat behind his desk and motioned for Hank, his former campaign manager, now chief of staff, to have a seat. The two men sat and looked at each other. The silence and tension grew as each waited for the other to speak first.

"The media will be onto a different story in a few days," Hank said. "I think we just wait it out."

"I don't want to drift off into the background. How do we recapture the initiative?" Duke picked up a football he had kept from his college days and tossed it a few inches into the air. "Defense is important, but the fans pay to see offense."

"Infrastructure, education, jobs, those are always popular," Hank said. "You could announce some new initiatives."

"That is all old hat. The public doesn't care about the nuts and bolts of governing. Besides, the payoff on those is long-term. Some future governor would get the credit. We need to retake the initiative. We need something to scare them, make them feel threatened, something only a strong leader can save them from."

"Your law and order approach isn't working anymore. Kicking down doors and arresting drug dealers has the public nervous. They are beginning to wonder if they are next." Hank flipped through videos on his phone and held one up so Duke could see it. "This is trending. It's a video of police arresting a sixty-eight-year-old cancer patient because she had some edibles and no medical marijuana card. This is why you won by less than a point."

"I see what you're saying. Those bloody idiots. But I think law and order can still work. We just need to shift the focus to violent crime. Carjacking, armed robbery, murder, rape, that type of thing. We should be able to do something with that." Duke put the football down and paced behind his desk.

"If people feel unsafe on the streets and in their homes, then they see a violent criminal getting arrested every few days, that should switch the law and order narrative back to positive."

"Easier said than done," Hank said. "But there is a lot of untested DNA evidence. Police have been collecting it from crime scenes but haven't had the funds to test it."

"I don't want to mess with old DNA evidence." Duke shook his head and stared out the window.

"Other states have done it. They end up solving a lot of cold cases. It will make great press. Hauling in criminals, the last Governor couldn't catch."

"Still, I would rather not. Can't we catch current criminals?"

"Sure, but those cases take a long time. And most of the credit will go to local law enforcement. It would look like you were taking credit for other people's work." Hank put his phone away. "A statewide cold case initiative would be all yours. You could appoint a task force and have him report directly to you."

"It seems messy. Digging through old DNA. You don't know what you will find."

"Rape and murder numbers are up. But there aren't enough of them to keep you in the news. It has to be the cases others couldn't solve. You would control it. If you find something you don't like, bury it. Actually, this gives you more control. You get first look at everything and can decide which cases to pursue."

"I would like to catch a few scum buckets. I miss standing before the cameras as they haul away criminals in handcuffs. Let's do it. But everything goes through me first. And I mean everything. And I want a task force I can control, no cowboys." Duke sat down. "I hope I'm doing the right thing. I hope this doesn't bite me in the ass. Hell, I've got my hands dirty before. If I need to, I can do it again."

29) DON'T BE RUDE

Stan sat down next to the brunette at the bar. She appeared to be in her mid-twenties, with a slim, athletic build. Stan thought, "She must jog. That's good. People should take care of their bodies. I hope she is nice. Not like most girls."

"Hi," Stan muttered.

The girl gave him a half-smile and turned away.

Stan dropped his head and thought, "That was rude. Please don't be stuck up. I don't want what happened to the other girls to happen to you. Why do I always pick the wrong girl? Why can't my relationships last? Mother was right."

"Can I buy you a drink?" Stan asked.

"No, I'm good." The girl waved to a guy on the other side of the bar and headed toward his table.

A dark fog entered Stan's mind. He thought, "Why do you have to be that way? Now you're going to make me do something I don't want to do. I promised myself I wouldn't do it anymore. I always promise myself, but I never keep my promises. I can't let another guy take my girl."

Stan sipped his beer and watched the girl out of

the corner of his eye. He could hear her giggle. Cold sweat ran down Stan's spine. A little after midnight, Stan paid his bill in cash, went to the parking lot, and sat in his pickup, watching the door. He munched on a half-eaten bag of potato chips. He licked his lips, tasting the salt.

A half-hour later, the girl appeared. The guy she was talking to was with her. She pointed down the street, then pointed left, giving him directions. Stan rolled down his window. She was speaking in a loud voice, slightly drunk. She repeated her address, and the guy walked toward his car.

The girl headed in the direction she had pointed, waved to the guy, and shouted, "See you soon."

Stan grabbed a screwdriver and walked purposefully toward the young man. As he got in his car, Stan said, "Hey do you have some jumper cables?"

"Shit. You scared me. No, I don't have any cables. Do people even jump cars anymore? Better call AAA."

"Sweet car. Is it a standard?"

"No, man." As the young man turned to get in the car, Stan inserted the screwdriver into the base of his skull. Stan caught the guy as he was collapsing. Opening the back door, he shoved him in and quickly checked to ensure he was dead.

"Hope you don't mind if I take it for a spin," Stan

said. "You're the twenty-fifth person I've killed. You don't get a prize or anything." Stan repeated the address he heard the girl give. It was about two blocks away.

"I was going to quit after the first one. Some other guy got convicted for that murder. It was such a kick watching the DA on TV. He was proud he had caught a murderer. I've been outsmarting them ever since." Stan stopped a few houses down and watched the girl go inside. "Look at me talking to a dead man. As they say, Dead men tell no tales. You know what is funny about that first case, do you? Oh yeah, I guess you're not in a talking mood. The DA is now the Governor. Yep, Duke Billings, that case made him famous. He owes it all to me."

Stan watched as the girl stepped out onto the porch and looked around. She shrugged her shoulders and left the door open.

"Looks like my girlfriend is lonely. You know she is my girlfriend, not yours. Sorry, I had to take your car. You are making a mess back there. But a little bleach should get the blood out. Make sure you wear gloves," Stan said. "I hope I don't have to kill her. I'm trying to stop. I always say afterward, no more. But then, a few months pass, and I'm back at it. You are an excellent listener. I should drive around with a dead man all the time."

Stan pulled out a knife and checked the blade. "It's important to keep the blade sharp. I really don't want to do this. I tried to pick up women the normal way. You know the way you do it. Some guys make it look so easy. I even bought this book on pickup lines. Total waste of twenty dollars. I guess I shouldn't keep her waiting. Don't want to be rude."

27) DNA REVISITED

The front wall was glass, so anyone could see the important investigation work being done. The back wall had a large map of Ohio, with pushpins scattered throughout. Red yarn connected a few, and others were joined by yellow. The map was a new edition; it had been put up when a disturbing tread had been spotted.

Staring at the map, Robert Stern poured another cup of coffee. He did not need the caffeine to keep him awake; his adrenaline would accomplish that. The pattern of the crime scenes alone was enough to suggest a serial killer was on the loose. How has no one noticed this?

The recent horrific crime, where a woman was murdered and raped in her home, and a second man was found dead in the backseat of his car, was the latest. The DNA from that murder matched three others. He also suspected that another four murders would match once the DNA results were returned from the lab.

What troubled Stern was the Jake Franklin case. It fits the profile, but the DNA was never entered into the crime database. He had to obtain a copy of Franklin's DNA from the defense attorney who had represented him during his trial. And on a hunch, had the crime scene DNA retested. The two samples did not match. Even more troubling was the DNA from the crime scene matched the serial killer.

Stern questioned the attorney as to why he never had it retested. The attorney danced around the question and never gave a clear answer. Stern could tell Franklin did not receive competent representation within ten minutes of talking to the attorney. It was highly likely that Jake Franklin, who has been in prison for the last eight years, is not guilty of rape and murder.

There was another case shortly after Franklin was convicted, it fits the profile, but the DNA evidence was never tested. The lab claimed that the sample was corrupted, but Stern had it retested. It matched the serial killer's DNA. This was no coincidence; two DNA samples from the same lab, in a short period, both botched. Someone had tampered with the evidence, but why?

When Stern took this position, he expected to pull murderers off the street. He didn't think he would find corruption within the legal system. But it was unmistakable; there were two cases where someone tampered with the DNA evidence. Someone in the criminal justice system is responsible for sending an innocent man to prison and allowing a murderer to run free.

Stern did not understand what type of person could have done this. Not only was an innocent man convicted of a horrendous crime. But it allowed a serial killer to remain free to kill again, which has apparently happened multiple times. The killings always involved a home invasion, in which a young female was raped and murdered, along with anyone else unfortunate enough to be in the house.

Stern was head of the cold case task force and reported directly to the Governor. The Governor had stated on multiple occasions that all findings were to be brought to him first. He was emphatic about it, almost paranoid. The trouble was that District Attorney Duke Billings had prosecuted the Franklin case, now the Governor and Stern's boss. There was definitely a conflict of interest.

Stern sipped his coffee and thought, "*Of course, the Governor doesn't know someone tampered with the DNA evidence. It has to be some low-level employee who botched the test and tried to cover his tracks.*"

Legally, not to mention common sense, says the Governor has to be hands-off on this one. A man's freedom is at stake. There can be no hint of misconduct. Stern's responsibility for law and justice had to come first.

But the Governor was clear. Under all circumstances, Stern was instructed not to proceed with an investigation until the Governor approved and signed off. Stern believed in the chain of command. The Governor had a right to run the task force how he saw fit. But Stern had also taken an oath to uphold the law. He had spent his life fighting for justice. And while Stern did not believe the Governor covered up the DNA, he was involved. It was simple, a person involved in the case cannot be the person in charge.

Stern knew the Governor. Sometimes he can be stubborn. He had a tendency to believe the rules did not apply to him. Stern had to find a way to inform the Governor but remove him from the case. The Governor wouldn't like it, but ultimately it was in his best interest.

Stern pored over the cases and noticed two occurred near the state border. Is it possible that the killer could have crossed state lines? He searched the cold cases from the neighboring state and found one that matched the killer's pattern. The serial killer was now a national problem. Stern put in a call to the FBI.

28) STERN

Duke Billings was sitting at his desk doing paperwork when Robert Stern poked his head through a crack in the door. "Robert, you wanted to see me. Please have a seat." Billings pointed to a chair in front of his desk. "I hope you have some good news. We are spending a lot of money testing old DNA kits, and so far, all you have solved is one old rape case."

"It takes time, sir," Stern said. "But we have identified a serial killer."

Billings put down his pen and sat up straight. "Really. How many murders?"

"We have firm DNA matches on four. Including the double murder that happened last month. There are another five that are almost certainly his, and maybe more."

"Excellent work." Billings' eyes lit up. He was thinking about all the press coverage a statewide manhunt would generate. He could do remotes from different parts of the state. Be seen comforting victims' families. This was a goldmine. "I'll get the State Police working on catching this scum bucket."

"Sir, his killing spree crosses state lines. So, I alerted the FBI."

Billings' head jerked around, and he stared at Stern. "I told you to come to me first. Those bastards are going to take the credit. Shit. This is a national story. The press is going to be unbelievable. You just screwed me, Stern. Instead of me being in front of those cameras, it will be some FBI stiff. Why can't anyone follow orders? "

"There is something else." Stern stood up and straightened his jacket. "The DNA matches the murder and rape from the Jake Franklin case."

"What? The piece of shit that murdered a guard. Are you trying to tell me the killer is already in prison?"

"No, I'm saying the wrong person is in prison."

Billings stood and turned toward his bookshelf. He pulled an old law book from his college days and leafed through the pages. "I thought you had something."

Billings turned back and faced Stern. "Drop the whole case. Call the FBI and let them know you made a mistake."

"I can't do that. I believe that evidence in the Jake Franklin case was tampered with. Someone is involved in a coverup. Maybe more than one person. We are going to need to do a full, independent investigation."

"That won't be necessary. I handled that case myself. I can assure you Jake Franklin was given a fair trial. Your job is to solve old cases. Not revisit ones that have been closed for years."

"Sir, I have to follow the evidence. I believe an innocent man is in jail."

"Innocent, he killed a prison guard."

"I can't speak to that. But the DNA evidence was incorrect. Any judge is going to throw that conviction out. And there is strong evidence that his first case involved a coverup."

"Are you accusing me of something?"

"No, sir. But since you are associated with this case, you must recuse yourself."

"This is my task force. I'm not doing any such thing," Billings said. "You're out. Go back to whatever job you were doing before. I'll find someone who can follow orders to lead the task force."

"You can't do that. It would be obstruction of justice."

"You little shit. Get out of my office."

Stern stared at Billings. For the first time, it crossed his mind; this may not be a low-level employee hiding his tracks. The Governor might know the DNA had been tampered with. Why else would he react this way? A cold chill ran through Stern's body. There would be a lot of pressure to cover this up. If Stern stood firm, his career would be ruined.

Stern's mind was racing. Governor Duke Billings had built his political career on law and order. Now he may have committed a major crime. One that cost a man his freedom. Stern had believed in the Governor. He had voted for him and attended his fundraisers. When his teenage daughter called Governor Billings a heavy-handed lying thug, he had lectured her for an hour and refused to loan her his car for a week. All of that was crashing before his eyes.

"Governor, were you aware that the DNA in the Franklin case was tampered with?"

Billings' face grew red. "How dare you ask me that. You can't come into my office and throw around accusations."

"You're right, sir. I was wrong to ask you that question here in your office. We need to do it in a legal setting. Sir, I'll need to get a deposition from you."

"Get out. Stern, you are done."

29) BLAME

The country estate was on one-hundred and sixty primarily wooded acres. You had to pass through two security checkpoints to reach the main house. The first was fifty yards after turning onto the driveway. Three guards were stationed in a small building. Two of them checked your car and verified you had legitimate business. The third guard carried an assault rifle and watched from a distance.

Once you reached the house, several aggressive dogs surrounded your car and kept you in place until a guard escorted you to the house. The entire process was designed to intimidate the average person and give the Governor the upper hand. Of course, if you were a VIP, you came by helicopter and missed the show.

Duke Billings met Todd Baker at the door and escorted him to the library. The room had no windows, and one wall had an enormous stone fireplace surrounded by bookshelves made of walnut. The other walls featured oil paintings of various hunting scenes. They sat in oversized leather chairs. A German Shepherd lay at Duke's feet. Hank, Duke's chief of staff, sat on the other side of the room. Duke poured a bourbon for Todd and one for himself. They both took a small sip and smiled at each other.

"Nice home," said Todd as he looked around the room. He went to put his drink down but noticed there wasn't a coaster and held it in his hand. Todd was surprised Duke invited him to his home, but he knew this was not a social visit.

"Is this the first time you have been here?" asked Duke. "I'll have to have you over more often. Do you hunt?"

"I saw the news," Todd said and sat his drink down. "You're not pinning this on me."

"Relax," Duke said. "This is a friendly meeting. I want to see If I can help you. After all, you were the one who screwed up the DNA test." Duke grabbed a coaster from an end table and placed Todd's drink on it.

"I came to you, and you did nothing. I may be guilty, but so are you." Todd's face grew red, and his hands trembled.

"Todd, how is your drug problem? I heard you went to rehab." Duke leaned back in his chair, sipped his bourbon, and studied Todd.

"I don't do drugs. That was a one-time incident." Todd leaned forward, reached for his drink, then pulled his hand back.

Duke shrugged, took another sip, and said, "I heard you tested positive for heroin. A little pot, I can understand. But heroin?"

"It was fentanyl. And I didn't know it was in the coke. I think someone set me up." Todd glanced at Duke. Todd had only done coke that one time. He was new at his job in Mexico, and his coworkers took him out on the town. He was drunk, and when they put the coke in front of him, he gave in to peer pressure and snorted a little.

"My apologies. A coke addiction can impact your work performance. But I think people understand addiction and are more tolerant nowadays. The important thing is that you got the help you needed."

"You're not pinning this on me. If I go down, you go with me."

"All you have to do is admit it was your mistake. And that I had no part. You didn't tell me because you didn't want to lose your job. Blame it on your drug use. People will understand."

Todd leaned back in his chair and stared at Duke. "No."

"You will get a year, maybe eighteen months. You will be out in six. I'll make sure a sympathetic judge hears your case. You will be sent to one of those country club prisons. I understand they have tennis courts."

"No."

"There will be a high-paying job waiting for you." Duke smiled at Todd.

"I don't trust you. I do this, and you leave me hanging. If we are both on the hook, you'll find a way to make the whole thing disappear."

"You forget, your incompetence caused this in the first place. You're the one who gave false testimony. One way or another, you are going to prison. Be smart and take the minimum security. You wouldn't last two days in a maximum security prison."

"If I go down, so do you."

Duke reached down and scratched his dog's neck. The dog sat up and licked Duke's hand.

"Do you own a dog? Amazing creatures. Loyal to a fault. Of course, I take good care of them. Plenty to eat, a nice warm, safe place to sleep. Everything they could want or need."

"I'm a cat person."

"Consider my offer. If you change your mind, let me know. But don't take too long," said Duke, his smile replaced by a stern look. "Hank, please show Mr. Baker the way out."

Baker stood up and followed Hank out the door. Hank offered his hand to shake, and Todd reluctantly took it. Todd's palm was moist from sweat. "We all know you will do the right thing,"

Hank said.

Hank returned, poured himself a bourbon, and sat across from Duke. "I guess we expected that would be his response."

"It figures the little puke would be a cat person."

"What do you want to do?"

"He has been a pain in my ass for too long," Duke said as he took a long sip of his bourbon. "Spread the word about his drug addiction. Also, rumors about how he suffers from depression."

"Should I contact our friend?" asked Hank. "Give him the go-ahead."

"Christ. Why couldn't Todd Baker be smarter? I'm giving him his only way out. A lousy six months in a minimum-security prison."

"If he was smarter. You would never have gotten into this position." Hank sipped his bourbon.

"How much political blowback are we going to get?"

"The opposition will be all over this. They will try everything to pin it on you. But we can convince our supporters it is a political hit job. The hard-core supporters will be with you matter what. It comes down to the independents. Like always, you have to make them hate the other guy more than they hate you."

"Independent voters. Shit why can't they take a

side? Let's poison the well. Keep them home on election day," Duke took a sip of bourbon. "Tell our friend it must look like suicide. But first, tell him to force Todd to make a video with a full confession. One that says he acted alone. Make sure his cat is in the video. If that doesn't say he is a sneaky little shit, I don't know what will. Hopefully, this puts an end to it."

30) TRUE CONFESSION

It was a Saturday night, and Todd was returning home from a basketball game. An acquaintance who had something 'come up' had given him the tickets. It had been an exciting game, and Todd was in a good mood. As he walked toward his small one-bedroom apartment, he pretended he was shooting the winning basket. He raised his arms and cheered for himself as the imaginary shot swished through the net.

Todd lived in an end unit with an outside staircase leading to his second-floor apartment. As he entered, a man stepped out from behind the door, placing his large rough hand over Todd's mouth. Another man was sitting on Todd's couch, pointing a pistol with a silencer at Todd. He put his finger to his lips and signaled for Todd to be quiet. At the same time, he turned up the volume on the TV.

"My name is John, and the scary-looking man over there is Henry. I'm going to take my hand off your mouth. Don't say a word."

"Help," Todd screamed.

The man punched Todd in the face. "Not a word. If someone hears you, we are going to kill them and you. Understand?"

Todd shook his head, and the man forced him to sit in front of a video camera.

The man on the couch got up and came over and lifted Todd's head, examining the area John had punched.

"Christ, John. That's going to leave a mark," said Henry. "Todd, settle down. This is a friendly visit. We need you to make a short video for us. Explaining how you alone are responsible for the DNA tampering."

"No way. I'm not taking the blame," Todd said. "Did Billings send you? Tell him to forget it."

"Todd, you need to understand that we are not taking no for an answer," Henry said.

"What are you going to do? Kill me?"

"If we have to. But there is a better way." Henry opened a briefcase filled with hundred-dollar bills. "That is one million dollars. Plus, we have a private plane to take you to the Marshall Islands."

Henry took a pack of bills out and tossed it to Todd. Todd thumbed through the bills and looked at John and Henry. The two of them smiled at Todd.

"One million? Why the Marshall Islands?" Todd

asked.

"No extradition. And a million dollars goes a long way there. You live out your life in safety and comfort." Henry took the pack of bills and returned it to the suitcase.

"What do I have to do?"

"Look into the camera and explain how you screwed up the DNA on the Jake Franklin case. How your drug problem has ruined your life. That you acted alone. Tell them you can't go on and have decided to take your own life."

"No way. Forget it. I say that, and then you kill me. I'm not an idiot." Todd said. "Get out of my apartment."

"Look, it's better for everyone concerned if we don't have to kill you," Henry said.

"Especially you," John said. He gave Todd a light tap on the back of the head.

"But if we have to, we will. We have this typed suicide note to use if you don't cooperate. It's not as good as getting you on video, but it will do. Plus, it will save us a million dollars. Your choice."

"Why do I have to fake my suicide? Why can't I just disappear?"

"The suicide is so they don't go looking for you. We have it all worked out. You're seen on a security camera taking a small boat out onto Lake Erie. When you're out of sight of land, we pick you up and leave the boat to drift."

"They will look for a body."

"That boat will drift for days. They won't know where to look."

"You said the Marshall Islands doesn't have extradition. That should be good enough. I'll do the video. But forget about the fake suicide."

"They can still interview you. We want it to be clean. Besides, you will be starting a new life. Isn't it better to leave the old life behind?"

"I want two million."

"Don't get greedy. But we figured you would be a tough negotiator. So we are going to throw in a beach house. We purchased this house. It will be all yours."

Henry handed Todd a picture of a small but idyllic house on a white sand beach.

"I get this house? And I never hear from you or Governor Billings again?"

"Just look into the camera, hit the record, and make the video."

It took three takes before Henry was satisfied with the video. To make it realistic, he insisted Todd snort coke on camera. Todd did not know it was laced with a lethal dose of fentanyl.

On the last take, Henry left the camera running. It recorded Todd's confession and his suicide by

STEVE LANCE

overdose.

31) UNDER PRESSURE

Duke stared out across a sea of reporters. The news had broken that there was a serial killer on the loose. The number of expected cases was up to twelve, including the Jake Franklin case. Duke had called the press conference to address the apparent suicide of Todd Baker.

At first, the news did not make much of an impression. One person was falsely imprisoned due to a faulty DNA test. It got some press but not much. Then the number of murders that could be attributed to the serial killer grew, with it, the press's interest in the case. With Todd Baker's suicide, it has reached a fever pitch. Billings had to get ahead of the story. It will not be long before a reporter puts all pieces together and ask difficult questions. Questions Billings does not want to answer.

Duke stepped to the microphone and said, "Todd Baker committed suicide rather than answer for his misdeeds. I am as shocked as you to learn he had fabricated DNA evidence. We are looking at all of his other work and retesting any DNA where he was involved in the case."

"Governor, did you know the DNA evidence was incorrect?" asked a reporter.

This was the first time Billings was asked directly if he knew of the tainted DNA evidence. It was bound to happen, and Billings was surprised it took this long. The plan was for Duke to go on the attack, never give an inch.

"No. I only found out because I assembled a task force to test and retest all DNA evidence. My task force not only identified the misdeeds of Todd Baker but identified a serial killer. A serial killer that the state police will soon find an arrest."

"Governor, you prosecuted the Franklin case. Why did you not question the DNA?"

"Todd Baker left a full confession. He explains how he deceived me, the judge, the jury, and the entire American Legal System. If someone in a position of trust is determined enough, they can hide their mistakes. Fortunately, the task force I created uncovered this malfeasance. Under my guidance, we will return integrity to a legal system the previous administration left in shambles."

"Governor, in Baker's video, there were bruises on his face. Some people are saying his confession was coerced."

"I'm sure that's what the media wants you to

believe. Conspiracy theories are good for the ratings. Well, I believe the Earth is round, and we landed on the moon. The same as I believe Baker went to great lengths to hide his incompetence." Duke smiled and said, "Although I'm not sure about Big Foot." A wave of laughter spread out over the press.

"Governor, will you be granting Jake Franklin a pardon?"

"Jake Franklin is a cold-blooded killer. In prison, he killed an inmate and a guard. He deserves to be on death row."

"Governor, if he had not been wrongly convicted, he never would have been in prison."

"Who says he was wrongly convicted? Franklin was tried and convicted of rape and murder by a jury of his peers. There was more evidence in his trial than just the DNA. It seems he was not the only one at the murder scene, but that does not mean he is innocent. He must have been working with the serial killer. Maybe he was the serial killer's mentor."

"Governor, a court is sure to overturn his original conviction. You know he didn't get a fair trial."

"He did get a fair trial. Once we catch the Franklin serial killer, I think we will find the extent of his involvement. I'm proud that I put away this man who apparently trained this new serial killer. If Todd Baker had told the truth, we could have caught and convicted both perpetrators."

"Governor, you called him the Franklin Serial Killer. Do you believe Jake Franklin trained him?"

"We are looking into the possibility. That's all the time I have. I need to go do the People's work."

The reports continued to shout out questions. Duke smiled, waved, and walked away.

32) BILLINGS

Back in his office, Duke Billings paced in front of the window. He watched as the last press trucks packed their gear and pulled away. A taped copy of the press conference played on a large TV screen. Billings had watched it twice before turning the sound down and running it for a third time.

Duke pointed to a reporter on the screen and said, "Make sure his press credentials are revoked. I didn't like his attitude."

Hank nodded, replacing the press conference with Todd Baker's taped confession and suicide.

Duke glanced at the screen and said, "How did those bruises get on Baker's face? I don't mind our guy roughed him up a bit, but doesn't he know enough not to leave marks where the camera can see them?"

"He took a personal dislike of Baker and got carried away," Hank said. "I talked to him. He feels bad about it."

"He should. I thought we were dealing with a professional. Not some amateur who can't control his emotions," Duke said. "Do you think the name

Franklin Serial Killer will stick?"

"I don't know if you played that right, sir," Hank said. Hank poured two bourbons and put one down on the Governor's desk. He was hoping this would get Duke to stop pacing and sit down. The last thing he wanted was someone with a telescopic lens to film the Governor looking worried.

"What do you mean?" Duke asked as he moved to his desk and looked down at the drink.

"You should have put it all on Todd and encouraged a judge to vacate the first conviction. Franklin is still on death row for killing the guard."

"I don't want people thinking I convicted an innocent man."

"You made him a major part of the story. The story is going to be he is involved with the serial killer. Jake Franklin will be in the news every day for a while. You could have just let him fade into the background. In a week, nobody would have cared about him."

"Shit." Duke sat down and took a sip of his bourbon. He knew Hank was right. It was a rookie mistake. You should always control the narrative.

"What happens when the serial killer is caught and says he acted alone? That he has no connection to Jake Franklin. It's not unusual for these killers to want full credit for their crimes."

Duke stared into space and said, "You better make sure he is not taken alive. Christ, why can't I get a break?"

33) STAN

Stan sat at a corner table. Billings press conference was playing, and all the bar patrons were watching. Stan's mood soured as the press conference went on. He hated that Billings called him the Franklin Serial Killer. Claiming that Franklin trained him. That the two of them committed the first murder. He would never do that. When he went on a date, it was always just him and the girl. If anyone else was around, he got rid of them so that he and his girl could have quality time alone. He wasn't some pervert; he didn't do threesomes.

Stan wanted to send a message, to tell people he always acts alone. Let them know why he does it and that he is only looking for the right woman. So they can settle down and start a family. That's the only reason he is doing this. He only killed the other woman because they were wrong for him. He had to kill them so they didn't go to the cops. Also, most of them were rude. One bit him. What would you do if someone bit you?

He watched as a young female reporter summarized the press conference. She seemed very professional. The type that would stick to the facts. Tell the truth. Maybe she would interview him. It would be good if people knew the truth. Then they would understand why he had to kill the women. How it wasn't something he was planning to do for the rest of his life. Only until he finds the right girl and they settle down and start a family. Everybody has the right to find happiness.

He listened to her sign-off, "This is Mary Johnson, reporting from the state capital." Stan wasn't far from the capital. He paid his bill and took off.

Stan waited at the television station. He had gone to the capital and saw Mary get in a TV remote van with another man. They then stopped at a restaurant. Stan wasn't hungry, so he waited for them back at the station. It was getting late, and most employees were gone for the day. He checked his Glock 19. It was fully loaded. He rarely used handguns; he felt knives were more personal. But this job called for one. Stan thought, *"The right tool for the right job."*

The parking lot had reserved spaces for the vans. They were all filled except for one. A large dumpster was off to the side. It was a perfect hiding place. Stan sat on the ground, out of sight.

He felt his stomach rumbling and wished he had stopped for some dinner. *"Maybe they will have a doggie bag,"* Stan thought.

It was dark by the time the van pulled in. Mary and the driver were laughing. Stan felt jealous. He wished he had someone to laugh with. He would have to put those feelings aside. Today was about business, not going on a date. This was purely professional. And as long as everyone did what they were told, nobody would get killed.

Stan pulled on a mask as Mary opened the door and rushed to the van. He put the Glock to Mary's head. "Back inside, he said." Stan jumped in behind them and pointed the gun at the driver. He ordered Mary back in her seat and put a rope around her neck. He pulled, so she sat straight up. Stan took two clear plastic zip ties and ordered the driver to fasten his hands on the steering wheel.

"Ten o'clock, two o'clock," Stan said, pointing to the location on the steering wheel. "Remember what the Driver's Ed teacher told us."

"Mary, you fasten one hand to the door handle, the other to the gearshift," Stan said. "You will have to shift for him. What's your name?"

"Roger. What do you want?"

"For you guys to do an exclusive. Now drive, head

north. We need to make the eleven o'clock," Stan said. "Sorry, I had to do it this way. But I need you to put me on TV."

"Let us go. You can have the van," Mary said.

"No, I don't want the van. I want you guys to do the broadcast for me. I saw you at the press conference, and there are a few things I want to straighten out." Stan smiled. "I'm the one who killed those people."

"You're the Franklin Serial Killer?"

"No. I hate that name. Could you come up with a better name for me?"

"Are you going to kill us?"

"No. Of course not. This is business. We are not on a date." Stan shook his head in disbelief. "Roger will work the camera, and Mary, you will interview me. If you were my date, I would have already killed Roger for moving in on my girl. What did you guys have for dinner?"

"Chinese."

"I know it was Chinese. I saw you pulling into the restaurant. What did you order?"

"Szechuan chicken."

"Oh, you should have gotten Hunan chicken

instead. It has the baby ears of corn."

"We will get that the next time."

"Yeah, you will like it. Hunan has better vegetables." Stan motioned for Roger to take the next turn. "Have you come up with a name for me?"

"How about the Woman Slayer?" asked Roger.

"That's awful. I don't slay women. Sometimes the date doesn't go very well, and I have to, you know," Stan said. "Pull off here."

"How about the Passionate Predator?" Mary asked.

"The Passionate Predator. Hmmm, that's better. But I'm not really a predator," said Stan. "Okay, pull into the grassy area, and let's do the interview."

They pulled into a large field, and Roger worked on setting up the satellite uplink. Mary did her best to fix her hair and makeup. When she finished, Stan motioned that she had a small smudge on her lips. Mary fixed it and thanked Stan.

"Can I call the station? Let them know we are going to do a live interview?" Mary asked.

"It's only nine o'clock. Won't they want to wait until the eleven o'clock news to air it?"

"Don't worry. They will do a special report."

"I didn't count on that," Stan said. "My favorite show is on at nine. I have my VCR set to tape it. I hate to miss it."

"This way, you will get a tape of your interview."

"Your smart. We should go on a date sometime."

"Remember, we are keeping this purely professional. We don't want people to think I soft balled the interview."

"You're right. I wish we had met under different circumstances. Okay, let's do the interview," Stan said.

"This is Mary Johnson coming to you live with a special report. We have a live interview with the serial killer known as the Passionate Predator." Mary held the microphone out. "What do you want to say to the public?"

"I saw Governor Billings' press conference today, and he made several errors. I alone was responsible for the killing in the Jake Franklin case. Franklin had nothing to do with it. He never entered the house. He dropped the young lady off and waited for her to go inside. Which was very gentlemanly of him. Then he drove away. Had he gone into the house, I would have killed him first. Check the other cases. That's always what I do."

"Are you saying Jake Franklin is innocent?"

"Yes. I watched the two of them in the bar. She got drunk. I think it was her birthday. He wasn't drinking at all. I remember because killing people is harder if they are not drunk. And I was thinking I was going to have to kill him. I mean, a guy takes a drunk girl home. He usually goes inside. But Jake dropped her off, not even a kiss goodnight, and drove away. Otherwise, he would be dead."

Mary's phone call enabled Billings' task force to get the location. As Mary continued with the interview, they were speeding in that direction.

After 30 minutes, Stan ended the interview. "Thank you. Sorry, I had to kidnap you. As promised, you're free to go."

At that moment, five police vehicles came rushing in. Roger had put the equipment away but turned on the phone camera.

Stan saw he was surrounded and tossed his Glock aside. He dropped to his knees and put his hands behind his head.

The first bullet caught Stan's right shoulder, the second one his left. Two head shots causing part of his skull to fly off followed. The task force pumped forty-three bullets into him.

Mary and Roger recorded the interview, but it was not broadcast. The task force confiscated the tapes, claiming they were evidence.

Several days later, Roger posted his phone video of Stan being shot while surrendering. Nobody cared that the police shot an unarmed man. They were happy the serial killer was dead.

34) VACATED

It was a typical courtroom, with the Judge sitting behind a large desk, high above everyone else. It spoke of his authority, designed to give off an air of infallibility. At the next level and to the right was the jury box. Honored guest to the proceedings. They were to remain silent, only to listen and observe, and at the end, to pass judgment. A simple guilty or not guilty. Their duty done, they would melt back into society. At the lowest level, front and center was the defendant. Lawyers on both sides would engage in verbal combat. And if everyone did their job and upheld themselves to the highest standards, truth, and justice would emerge, at least in theory. It was an imperfect system set up by imperfect humans, but it was the best available.

On this day, the jury box was empty. Because before the judge was the question of if everyone did their job, if the highest standards were upheld, and if truth and justice prevailed. The judge and the judge alone would decide. Had the criminal justice system failed and cost a man his freedom? His job was to filter out the imperfections and restore the presumption of innocence.

Michael Crane and Jake Franklin rose as the Judge entered the courtroom. It was a non-verbal code, showing that they would defer to the judge's wisdom. He sat down and indicated for the rest of the room to sit. The courtroom had over a dozen reporters watching the proceedings.

The Judge slowly worked through a set of papers. Occasionally scribbling his name. He glanced up at Jake. "Jake Franklin, please rise."

Jake stood and waited as the Judge examined a few more papers. "Mr. Franklin, I am vacating the conviction against you due to the faulty DNA evidence. I am unhappy about this decision, but the law demands I make it. We all must follow the law, Mr. Franklin. No exceptions. However, this decision in no way affects your conviction for the murder of the prison guard. You are to be returned to prison to serve out that sentence. I believe you are on death row and will be executed for your crime. As I said, we must all obey the law."

The Judge slammed his gavel and left the courtroom.

Michael Crane patted Jake on the back. "You told me the DNA was not yours. I wish I had listened. But this should help reduce your death sentence to life in prison."

"Now you believe me on the DNA. But you still don't believe I killed that guard in self-defense."

"It's not if I believe you. It's what's possible. I would

not be able to get that overturned. The best I can do is save your life."

"Save my life? I live in a six-by-eight cell. I eat shitty food. If I'm lucky, I see the sun for one hour a day. Half the time, they make an excuse why I can't go outside. Guards are always trying to trip me. More than once, I've found cockroaches in my food. I'm pretty sure they spit in it, if not worse. You call this a life? Stop thinking that changing my sentence to life in prison is a success. If I had a choice between fifty more years of this or death, I would take death. The only thing that keeps me going is that someone with an ounce of integrity will blow the lid off this whole corrupt scam. Show that Billings, the warden, and the guards that testified against me are liars. That they should be in prison, not me."

"Our best bet is to follow the process. Take it one step at a time."

"How can you be so blind?" Jake asked. "Haven't you ever wondered why my death row case is moving at lightning speed while every other case is crawling at a snail's pace?"

"I figured it was because a guard was involved."

"Come on. You can do better than that. Half the death row cases involve the murder of a police officer. It's Governor Billings pushing it. He has something to hide, and he wants me dead."

"The Governor? Why?"

"He was the District Attorney on the original case. He knew the DNA evidence was faulty before I was convicted. He is trying to cover up his involvement. He probably had Todd Baker killed." Jake shook his head. "Now he is saying I'm involved with this serial killer. I'll bet you anything they won't take the real killer alive. They won't want him saying I had nothing to do with the first murder. And that we don't know each other."

"You're right," Michael said as he picked up his briefcase.

"About what?"

"They caught the serial killer. He was shot dead while resisting arrest. But it looks suspicious. There is a video of him with his hands behind his head."

"I'm on death row. All I did was protect myself when a guard and inmate entered my cell in the middle of the night. It was the third time I was attacked while in prison. Meanwhile, Governor Duke Billings is piling up bodies left and right."

"Come on, time to go. A prison guard is waiting to take you back," Michael said.

"Do I get to talk to the press?" Jake turned and watched as they filed out of the room.

"No. You're still a prisoner."

"You do it then. Tell them I'm an innocent man being railroaded by the Governor. Oh, and tell them they are doing a shitty job, and it's no wonder nobody listens to them anymore."

"How about If I just tell them you're innocent?"

"You're doing a shitty job too. Put that law degree to work. You're an officer of the court. Doesn't it bother you that an innocent man is in prison?"

"I do the best I can."

35) FLAT TIRE

Bob Wilkes, a guard from the prison, led Jake Franklin to the loading dock. Parked was a ten-seat white van with no side windows. Jake was the only passenger, and the guard's job was to return him to the prison.

It was early evening, and it had been raining most of the day. But the clouds were parting, and a few rays of sunshine made their way through.

Jake stepped over a puddle left on the pavement and asked, "Don't you guys usually work in pairs?"

"The other guard called in sick. And the prison didn't want to pay overtime." The guard put Jake in the van and fastened his seat belt. "If you give me any trouble, I'm supposed to shoot you. They mentioned that several times to me." The guard gave Jake a friendly smile. "Is that good? You comfortable?" Jake gave him a slight nod.

"I made my attorney give me twenty bucks. Any chance we can pick up a couple of milkshakes? My treat," Jake said.

Jake was playing head games with the guard. Prisoners often used this tactic, asking a guard to do something decent, to bend the rules in some small way. It was to remind the guard that they were still human beings. Most guards ignored the prisoners, but it got under the skin of a few.

"Sure, why not. It's a hell of a thing, being imprisoned for something you didn't do. Do you like chili dogs? I know a drive-through with the best dogs this side of the Mississippi."

Looking surprised, Jake responded, "That's decent of you. I didn't expect you to agree. I don't actually have twenty dollars. What's your name?"

"Bob. Bob Wilkes. My treat."

"Don't you mean Officer Wilkes, sir?"

"Hey, look. I'm not like that. Not like most of the guards," Bob said. "I know you were acting in self-defense when you killed that guard. He was a real piece of work. And now you didn't even commit the crime you were sent away for. It's a hell of a thing."

"Why haven't you said anything?"

"I don't actually know. I mean, I didn't see anything. I just know how it is. Nothing they claim makes any sense. I don't have any proof. If I did, I would speak up. Or at least I hope I would. In truth, I probably wouldn't." Bob got quiet, then said, "It's a hell of a thing."

"Yeah, you said that. Nobody saw anything. But here you are, driving a van with an innocent man in chains. What does that make you?"

"Hey, I'm just doing my job."

"Forget about those chili dogs. I lost my appetite."

Bob hated working at the prison. A prisoner says the wrong thing, and a fight breaks out. Look at someone wrong, and you can get stabbed. Show weakness, and you become someone's bitch. Everything was driven down to the lowest common denominator. The guards couldn't do anything. There were too few guards and too many prisoners. So, the prison gang leaders got special favors for making sure some level of order was kept. You can't blame the prisoners or the guards. It's the system. Create an environment of desperate men feeding on each other, and hell on earth evolves. Darwin would be right at home.

The last of the storm clouds dropped a few raindrops on the windshield. They drove in silence for over an hour before Jake said, "Bob. Thanks for offering to get those chili dogs. It was a decent thing to do."

"I've been thinking. They are going to execute you. You're on death row, and I've never seen anyone go through their appeals as quickly as you. I think what you are saying about the Governor is true. I keep going over it in my mind, and the only thing that makes sense is what you are saying. You are innocent of everything. You're just some dude who is getting chewed up by bureaucracy."

"A corrupt bureaucracy. One that is going to execute me."

"Do you think I'll go to hell for being part of it?"

"Absolutely."

"No, I'm being serious." Bob glanced back at Jake. Jake could see that Bob's eyes were glassy.

"If you saw a man dying. And you could save his life and didn't," Jake said. "What do you think the man upstairs would say? No, you are definitely going to burn in hell. You, the Governor, the warden, the whole damn lot."

"Don't say that. I know what is happing to you is wrong. I feel real bad about it."

"You're on the wrong team, Bob. The devil will march all of you right into a pit of sulfur. And don't think that you will be excused because you know it is wrong. That makes it worse. You know it's wrong, and you still do it. You're the devil's favorite type. A whining, bleeding heart who complains but goes along anyway. He is going to throw on a few extra chunks of coal for you."

"It's not like that. I'm just doing my job."

"I get it. You're following orders."

"Yeah. That's right."

"Just like the Nazis."

"Shut your mouth."

They drove for another hour before Bob said, "I've

been thinking. If I was to get a flat tire, I would make you change it." Bob glanced at Jake in the mirror. "Of course, I would have to take off your cuffs."

"Seems fair. After all, you have done all the driving."

"It's getting dark. Good chance if you made a run for it, I would have to shoot, but in the dark, I probably wouldn't hit you. I would give chase. You would have a good half hour by the time I got back and radioed it in." Bob glanced back, "Do you want to change a tire?"

"Hell yeah, I do," said Jake. "I take back the Nazi comment."

"I'll probably get fired."

"What do they expect? Sending one man out to handle a known killer."

"I don't think I can work there anymore. I've been thinking of getting a certification in welding."

"There is a high demand for welders. The pay is good too."

Bob wasn't sure why he was doing this. No one would know he let Jake go. They would assume he was just stupid and let him escape. Either way, he would get fired. Bob wondered if he was doing it for Jake or if it was a way to permanently end his job. He had tried to quit several times but always backed out at the last minute. Perhaps this was a way of making it, so he couldn't back out. Be done with a job he truly hated, once and for all. Maybe there is always a selfish reason for everything you do. Perhaps that is just how humans are.

Bob drove to a section of the highway surrounded by woods and pulled off. He took out his wallet and removed forty-eight dollars. He unshackled Jake and handed him the money.

"It's not much. But it may help."

"You're a good man, Bob. Don't forget to punch a hole in the tire."

"What happened to you. It's a hell of a thing."

36) ON THE RUN

Jake darted into the woods. He looked back at Bob Wilkes, who was placing a nail under his tire. Got in his van and drove over it. It had been a long time since anyone had been kind to Jake, let alone stick their neck out. They would undoubtedly fire Wilkes. Even though they may not find out he helped Jake, they would still fire him for letting Jake escape. Duke Billings would make sure of that. It was probably for the best.

A rush of adrenaline flowed through Jake. He was free, and it felt great. Jake held his hands out as he ran past a group of bushes. Water from the recent rain flew at him. It wasn't enough to wash away everything that had happened to him, but it was a start.

Wilkes said he would give him half an hour before reporting his escape. He would need a change of clothes, and with the little money he had, Goodwill seemed like the best choice.

Jake made his way through the woods until he came to a small town. It was late at night, so all the stores were closed. He saw a large metal donation box outside a grocery store. It was overflowing with plastic bags filled with donated clothes. He grabbed a couple of bags and headed back into the woods.

Two pairs of jeans fit him and several shirts. He changed and rolled the extra clothes into a blanket he found. He put the remaining clothes in plastic bags and returned to the donation container. It occurred to him that this was the first time he had ever stolen anything or, for that matter, committed any crime. And at best, this was a misdemeanor. But that didn't change the fact he was an escaped death row fugitive. It wouldn't be long before his picture would be on every television screen.

Jake knew where he had to go. He had read an article about it. The wealthy maintained hunting cabins in a sparsely populated wooded area about a hundred miles from where he was. They rarely used them, and the cabins remain vacant most of the year. It was a perfect hiding place.

It would take three days of walking. If he stole a car, he could be there in two hours. But stealing a vehicle was a felony. Jake didn't mind being a fugitive, but he drew the line at being a felon. Although what he was planning would switch the two.

A full-scale manhunt would be underway, and Jake's picture would be plastered everywhere. So, Jake kept to the woods. He used the roads to navigate but was careful to always keep out of view. After three days, he reached his destination. It was a nice size hunting cabin; some may even call it a lodge. He had recalled seeing pictures of this hunting lodge in a magazine that reported on the rich and famous. He knew the person who owned it would not use it for a while. It was deserted, but Jake decided to stay in the woods and watch it for at least a week. The manhunt would still be in full swing, and someone will probably check these cabins.

On his fourth day, he watched a sheriff's vehicle pull up to the cabin. The officer got out and walked around the cabin. He looked in several windows and examined the dust on the porch for any sign of recent activity. Jake had not gone near the cabin. The officer scanned the woods surrounding the cabin, looking straight in Jake's direction.

Any movement, sneeze, or cough would give Jake away. His heart was beating so fast he was sure it would be heard. Suddenly there was a rustling in the woods next to Jake. The officer reached for his sidearm. Out of the woods jumped a deer. It darted halfway across the yard, stopped directly in front of where Jake was hiding, and stared at the officer. The officer made his fingers into a gun and pointed it at the deer. Jake heard him say, "Bang. You're lucky it's not hunting season. But I guess you're safe for now."

The officer smiled and got back in the car. He

talked on the radio for several minutes before driving off.

Jake waited over an hour before deciding it was safe to approach the cabin. He checked all the windows; everything was locked up tight. The back porch had a broom which he used to sweep away his footprints. He scanned the rocks that led up to the front door and, one by one, turned them over. Finally, he found one that wasn't a real rock. It had a small latch on the bottom, and inside was a key.

37) MANHUNT

The cabin proved to be the perfect hiding place. It was a rarely used hunting lodge owned by a rich, influential person. The best part, the hunting lodge belonged to Governor Duke Billings. And the Governor was much too busy to visit. It was remote but still had all the modern conveniences, running water, power, and even the internet. It was well stocked with plenty of food and several cases of high-priced bourbon. Jake didn't drink any of the bourbon. Instead, he found enjoyment in using it for target practice. He did find a box of fine Cuban cigars. They were illegal to own, a direct violation of the US embargo against a communist regime. Jake decided to help Duke out by smoking the evidence.

Jake had developed a convincing disguise and would travel to a town about thirty miles away. There he rescued two German shepherds, which he named Ben and Bob. When walking through the shelter, he had an overwhelming desire to release all the dogs from their cages. It broke his heart when he lingered in front of a cage, and the dog's tail would raise slightly and slowly wag. The dog hoped this would be his turn to be taken home, fulfill his purpose, and become man's best friend. But Jake and the dog would only stare at each other with the same eyes, knowing that today was not the day.

Jake had to accept he could only rescue the two shepherds. Sometimes we are a disappointment to our heart. He wondered if that was how his death row lawyer felt. Undoubtedly, he had an overwhelming caseload. There were only so many he could rescue. And Jake had been the growling dog, snapping at people, mad at the world. Instead of the one with hope, holding out that man's better nature would prevail and he would be rescued.

But even before his life was thrown into chaos, he was never the type to rely on the kindness of strangers. He always believed you were responsible for your own life and nobody would help in any meaningful way. But he also believed that society was just and if you did the right thing, you would be treated fairly. He was naïve in his beliefs, but at the time, he had no frame of reference. He had not experienced what it meant to go up against a corrupt system. It pained him to remember who he was before the first trial; he was not only ignorant but willfully ignorant. When people would complain about the system, he would dismiss them, view them as malcontents. He did not search for the truth but instead embraced the one that fit his beliefs. In the end, it was Ben, his cellmate, who rescued his spirit, and Bob Wilkes, who opened the cage.

It had been six months since Jake's escape, and the manhunt was over. He was still a wanted man, but the world had moved on. The press had lost interest, and the Governor didn't want to remind people of the messy details; instead, Duke Billings was focused on rebuilding his image. He had successfully placed most of the blame on Todd Baker and used Jake's escape as more proof that he was a hardened criminal. You don't run if you have nothing to hide.

They crucified Bob Wilkes in the press. He was fired from his job and lost his health care and pension benefits. Jake saw a picture of him. Bob's eyes seemed brighter, and there was a faint smile. He would make a fine welder. Someone who built things.

Jake had become a student of Duke Billings, learning his every move. Where he went, what he ate, and who was with him. It turned out Billings was a man of habit. Very predictable. He had few friends, and the few he had gave him a wide berth. For Duke, everything was transactional. But don't expect him to uphold his side of the bargain.

Jake's cellmate Ben was a psychopath, but he had a code he lived by. He had committed a horrendous crime and was rightfully imprisoned. Ben himself would tell you that. He was not delusional. Ben understood right from wrong. Duke was also a psychopath, but he did not have a code. It is doubtful he even understood right from wrong. For Duke, if he won, it was proof he was right. If he lost, someone had screwed him.

The lodge had an ample supply of thick porterhouse steaks. Jake took three and headed to an outside grill. As the steaks cooked, Jake watched a hawk soar. Gliding effortlessly on the air currents. At one point, it swooped down and snatched a field mouse, then used its powerful wings to soar, flying off into the distance.

The two German Shepherds sat front and center, watching Jake put one steak on a plate. Their eyes were full of anticipation. Jake tossed the other two steaks at Ben and Bob. "If you were really Ben, you would complain that I overcooked your steak," Jake said. "Then tell me I'm a dead man if I go forward with my plan. Probably call me a dumbass." The shepherds paid no attention to Jake. They were too busy enjoying their meal. Jake envied their ability to live in the moment. They had put their time in the shelter behind them.

While Jake enjoyed sleeping in the Governor's bed, walking around the cabin wearing his robe, and eating his food, it was time to implement his plan. He had everything he needed, chloroform to knock Billings out, a quick-acting sedative to keep him unconscious. A vehicle with a large trunk. He had purchased it with money from selling Duke's hunting rifles. A room prepared to hold the Governor; the walls were covered with his campaign posters. Jake figured the campaign posters were a nice touch. Everyone likes to look at pictures of themselves. The room was uncomfortable, but Billings would not be there very long.

38) FORE

Jake arrived at the country club early in the morning. The dew was heavy on the grass, and the trees were full of chirping birds engaged in an early morning gossip session. He drove down a dirt road that ran the length of the backside of the golf course. The moisture in the air kept dust from rising. He pulled the car off into a flat grassy area and released the trunk latch but kept the lid down. He would need to access it quickly.

A ten-foot chain-linked fence separated the club members from the rest of the world. It was more a symbol than a barrier. The world was divided into many different groups, and everyone was expected to stay on their side of the fence.

Jake had cut a slit into the fence on a previous trip and mended it with fishing line before leaving. Using a sharp knife, he cut through the line and pushed the section of the fence open. He would leave it open, allowing him to make a quick get-a-way if needed. Jake made his way into the woods surrounding the course, being careful to stay out of sight and not make any noise. He staked out a position that allowed him to observe Billings as he played the fourth and fifth holes. Jake pulled out a pair of binoculars and chuckled at Duke's choice of slacks. Billings had gone with the old Scottish golfer look.

Billings played golf regularly but was not very good. He did not enjoy the game, but important business gets done on the golf courses, and Billings did not want to be excluded. The course he was playing had a dogleg on the fifth hole. It was common for Billings to drive his ball into the woods and spend five minutes or more looking for it.

Jake was a scratch golfer himself. It amused him to watch Billings play. He spotted several easily fixable flaws in Duke's game. He wondered if the people around him were too frightened to point out his shortcomings. Jake's biggest enjoyment was when Billings blamed the club and sent it flying. Jake thought, *"He must spend a fortune on golf clubs."*

Back at Duke's cabin, Jake had found one of his drivers and a few dozen balls. He had spent a pleasant afternoon driving them into a pond. Jake was going to miss the cabin. But at least he would get to see it one last time.

As the dew burned off the grass, the sun slipped behind dark clouds, rolling in from the north, bringing a chill to the air. The weather forecast called for storms later in the day, which were expected to last for the foreseeable future. Jake remained hidden in the woods. This was his third trip, and he hoped today would be the day Duke went looking for his ball. Duke was having a bad day; he was seven over par, but the scorecard read three over par. Honesty was not Duke's strong suit.

The drive off the tee was a big soring hook. A perfect shot. For Jake, that is. The ball went deep into the woods, and Duke chased after it. Jake spotted the ball and placed it where Duke would have a shot back to the fairway. As Duke lined up his shot, Jake stepped out from behind a tree and put a chloroform-soaked cloth over his nose and mouth. Duke struggled for a minute, then collapsed. Jake pulled out a syringe and injected him with a strong sedative. Duke went limp. He was a big guy, but Jake had practiced the best way to carry an unconscious person.

Throwing Duke over his shoulder, Jake carried him through the slit in the chain-link fence and shoved him into the trunk of a waiting car. The entire operation took less than two minutes. There was no need to seal up the cut in the fence. In a few minutes, it would be obvious what had happened.

Hank, his chief-of-staff and golf partner that day, got tired of waiting and hit his approach shot onto the green. He shouted, "Duke, you just missed a beautiful shot. I'm on in two."

Hank stared at the woods. "Just drop a new ball. Or

zip up, and let's go. I'll meet you at the green."

Hank and the security strolled around the green, glancing back at the spot Duke went into the woods. They were used to Duke taking a long time to find his ball. Duke was not one to willingly take a penalty stroke. But something seemed off today. Usually, you could hear the occasional cuss word coming from the woods. Today it was strangely quiet.

"You better go check on him," Hank told the security detail. "Don't let him cheat. It's a penalty if he loses his ball."

Duke's personal security detail went into the woods. A few minutes passed as Hank paced around the green. He then saw one of the security detail running out of the woods, speaking into his radio. The man jumped into a golf cart and drove toward Hank.

"The Governor is gone. There is a hole cut in the fence," the man said. "We have choppers on the way. And we found this note."

Hank read the note. *"Robert Billings has been charged with falsifying evidence, witness tampering, false imprisonment, and the murder of Todd Baker. The Honorable Jake Franklin will judge and sentence him. More details to follow."*

Hank reread the note, folded and put it in his pocket. "How the hell could you let this happen?"

"The Governor doesn't like people to follow him in the woods. He always tells us he lost the ball and he will find it. You know how he is."

"Shit, he only says that so nobody sees him cheat. Like it's a big secret that he cheats at golf. Or everything else, for that matter," Hank said. "What do we do now?"

"Sir, we have arranged for the State Police to escort you back to the capital. We have mobilized all law enforcement. Don't worry; we will find him."

"Don't let the press know. We have to come up with a plan first," Hank said.

"We put out an APB. The press knows."

"Damn, Jake Franklin. How can one man cause so much trouble?"

39) CONFESS

Duke woke to find himself handcuffed to a metal table. His campaign posters covered the walls. The room looked familiar, but he couldn't place it. Jake Franklin sat across from him, eating a bagel and drinking coffee from a mug that read 'The World's Greatest DA!'. The cup initially read 'The World's Greatest DAD,' but someone had used a black marker to change the last 'D' into an exclamation point.

"Good morning. Actually, it's early evening," Jake said. "Care for a bagel? When I was in prison, all we had was nasty old toast. With some type of spread, they pretended it was butter. There was a lot in prison that wasn't what it seemed."

"What am I doing here?" Duke searched the room for a clue to his whereabouts. He rattled the chain that was holding his handcuffs to the table.

"Do you like how the handcuffs are attached to the table? That is a trick I learned in prison. They do that so you can sit and have a nice conversation. Without the other person worrying, you may attack them."

"How did I get here?"

"Oh. You hit your ball out of bounds. I'm afraid you will have to take a penalty stroke. And people saw you, so you can't kick it back in and pretend it bounced off a rock. No cheating this time."

A realization crossed Duke's face. He said, "You're that murderer. Jake Franklin."

"Half right. I am Jake Franklin. And I'm looking at a murderer, so maybe three-quarters right." Jake took a swig of coffee, read the words on the mug, and held it up so Duke could see it. "You even falsified your mug."

"When they catch you, you are going to fry." Duke rattled his handcuffs. It did no good. He was securely fastened to the table.

"District Attorney Billings, you disappoint me. They don't use the electric chair anymore. It's lethal injection now. A kinder, gentler way to execute people. Personally, I think they should bring back hanging. I'm a no-mercy kind of guy. Which you are going to find out shortly."

"What, you're going to murder me? Like you murdered that guard."

"Governor, we are going to have to get our terms correct. I killed that guard. I killed him in self-defense. Not murder, killed. You, on the other hand, murdered Todd Baker. Not kill him; you had someone else do that. But because you ordered it, you are the one who murdered him. You were a District Attorney. I'm surprised you don't know this."

"In that case, you murdered that woman. It may not have been your DNA, but you were involved."

"Now you're just lying. And, of course, that's why you ordered the serial killer to be shot down before he could confess and clear my name," Jake said. "But, I'm glad you murdered him. The first woman he killed was a friend of mine. I am not a forgiving man. I'm happy he is dead. Also, I am not about to forgive you for accusing me of her rape and murder and falsely imprisoning me for eight years."

"You're going to murder me?"

"No. What I want from you is the truth. Just come clean on what you did, and you get to go home."

"You think I'm a fool? You're recording this. I'm not saying anything."

"Governor, I'm going to set aside the question of if you're a fool. I'll let other people decide that. And I'm not recording this. But I am streaming it live. Say hi to your fans. Go ahead, do a little fundraising."

Jake pointed to a camera perched in the top corner of the room. "Right now, we have twelve thousand people watching. But it is growing fast. And don't worry, if someone misses the live show, they can watch it later. So I guess you are right. It is being recorded."

"You're the fool. They can trace this transmission. You will be caught."

"Yes, they can. And the police will be here soon. But not before you tell the truth."

Jake pulled out a syringe and showed it to Billings.

"What is that? Sodium Pentothal? That is not admissible in court."

"This is not a court of law but a court of truth. Besides, It's not Sodium Pentothal. It is SP-117, which the KGB used as a truth serum. Very effective. Fast acting as well. You will be spilling your guts in a few seconds."

Jake approached Billings with the needle filled with SP-117. Duke jerked around, trying to keep Jake away. "Governor, you must settle down, or I'll have to tase you." Billings glared as Jake injected Billings with the truth serum.

Returning to his seat, Jake took a sip of his coffee. He looked into the camera and smiled. "It will only take a minute, and the truth will come out. If you're enjoying this broadcast, please hit the subscribe button. Personally, I think we should inject our politicians once a month, have them tell us the truth live on air."

Jake watched as Billings' head sank to his chin. "All right folks, he looks about ready. Let's do a test," Jake said, looking into the camera.

"Governor Billings, do you cheat at golf?"

"Hell yes. I even cheat when I don't have to. Nobody is going to dare challenge me. I'm the Governor; I can make their life a living hell."

Jake gave a thumbs-up to the camera. "Governor Billings, tell me about Todd Baker."

"That little shit. Tried to put the squeeze on me. He screwed up the DNA test. Almost cost me my biggest case. I told him to keep his mouth shut. Nobody needed to know I had the results before the trial was over. I tried to be reasonable. But he wouldn't listen. That's what I get for trying to help out."

"Governor, what happened to Todd Baker?"

"I had him killed. Serves him right. The people who did it said he shit himself. I wish I could have seen it. The little shit, shit himself." Billings chuckled to himself.

"Was Jake Franklin guilty of any crimes?"

"No, he was completely innocent. Boy, I did a number on him. I didn't mean to. At first, I thought he was guilty. When I found out he was innocent, it was too late. It would have ruined my career. I wouldn't be Governor. That guard was something else. I had to put the squeeze on the warden to get him to frame Franklin. Everyone is incompetent. The warden still had a tape showing Franklin acted in self-defense. I took it. It's in my office safe. Poor Franklin never had a chance. That's what you get when you mess with Duke Billings."

In the distance, Jake could hear the sound of a helicopter. There was no place to land; it would most likely be used to track anyone who fled the cabin. Jake had no plan to run.

Shortly after the chopper arrived overhead, several vehicles, sirens blaring, pulled up to the cabin. Jake had tethered the German Shepherds in the woods, out of the way of the police, but that didn't stop the dogs from barking. Fortunately, the police had the decency not to shoot them; I guess they figured the chopper was making so much noise it didn't matter. It's also a lot harder to shoot a dog than a human.

Jake posted photos of the two dogs next to the live feed. He hoped someone would adopt them, and they would not have to return to the shelter. It was the one part of his plan that wasn't solid. Sometimes you disappoint yourself, and others have to pay the price.

The live feed was cut, and Jake could hear the front door being kicked in and several sets of boots running from room to room. Every few seconds, he heard the word "clear" shouted. It would only be a few seconds before they found Jake with Billings.

Jake switched to a new live feed using his cell phone. He lay flat on the ground, arm spread wide.

Duke Billings' task force broke into the room, weapons drawn. Two of the members released

Billings and headed for the door.

Billings turned and shouted, "Shoot him! Kill that son of a bitch. He knows too much."

The remaining task force members opened fire and gunned Jake Franklin down in full view of the camera.

The End

Made in the USA
Monee, IL
16 August 2023